D1130602

A REALLY WEIRD SUMMER

Eloise Jarvis McGraw

A Margaret K. McElderry Book

ATHENEUM 1978 NEW YORK

For my technical advisors,

CHRIS AND BILLY,

with love

Library of Congress Cataloging in Publication Data

McGraw, Eloise Jarvis. A really weird summer.
"A Margaret K. McElderry book."
Summary: Four children in Oregon spend the summer
of their parents' divorce with a little-known
great aunt and uncle.
[1 Divorce—Fiction. 2. Oregon—Fiction] I. Title
PZ7.M1696Re [Fic] 76-28718
ISBN 0-689-50077-7

Published simultaneously in Canada by
McClelland & Stewart, Ltd.
Manufactured in the United States of America
by The Book Press, Brattleboro, Vermont
First Printing April 1977
Second Printing September 1978

CONTENTS

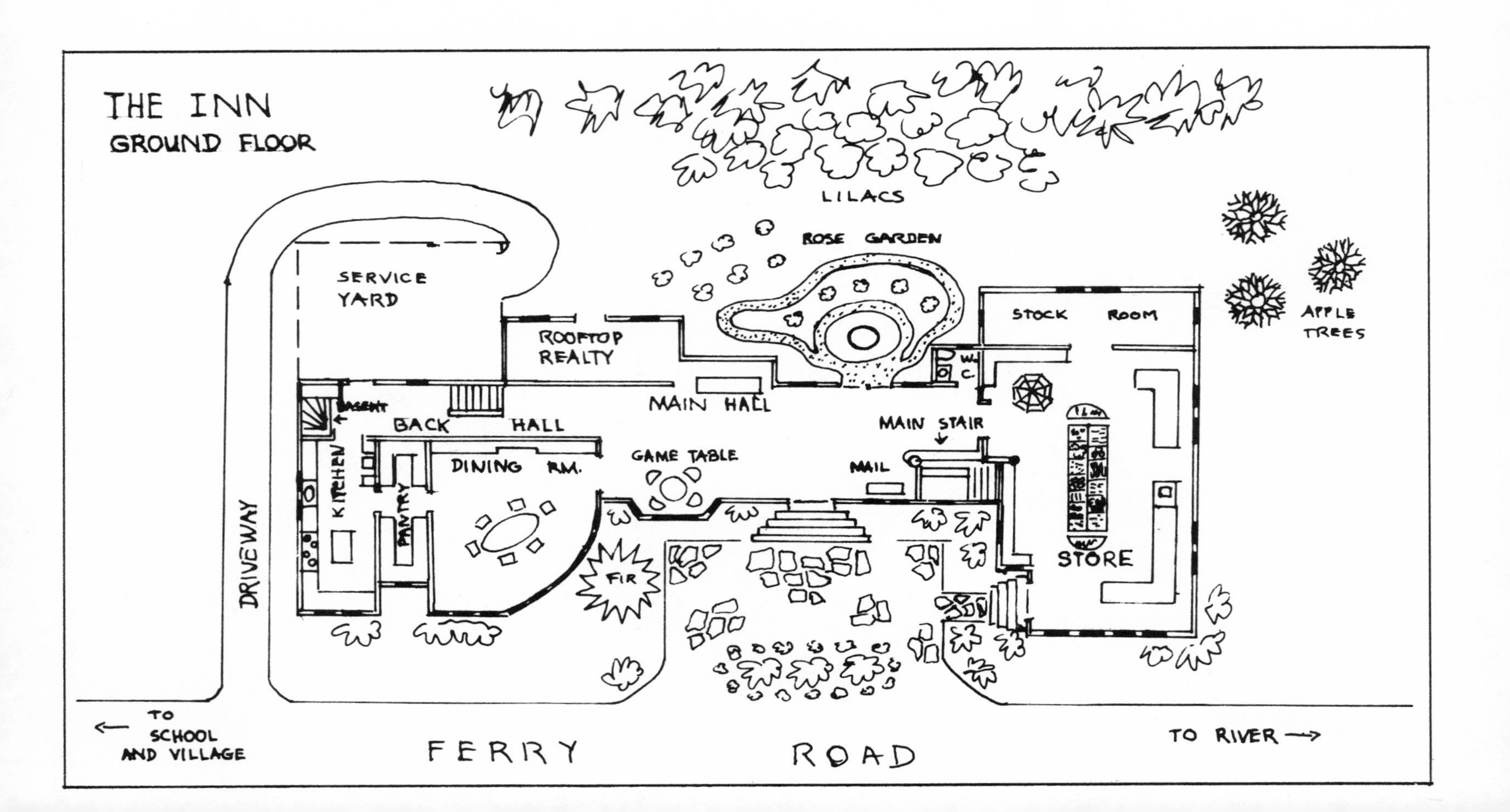
THE INN
GROUND FLOOR
LILACS
ROSE GARDEN
APPLE TREES
SERVICE YARD
ROOFTOP REALTY
STOCK ROOM
W. C.
MAIN HALL
BACK HALL
MAIN STAIR
GAME TABLE
MAIL
DINING RM.
KITCHEN
PANTRY
STORE
FIR
DRIVEWAY
TO SCHOOL AND VILLAGE
FERRY ROAD
TO RIVER

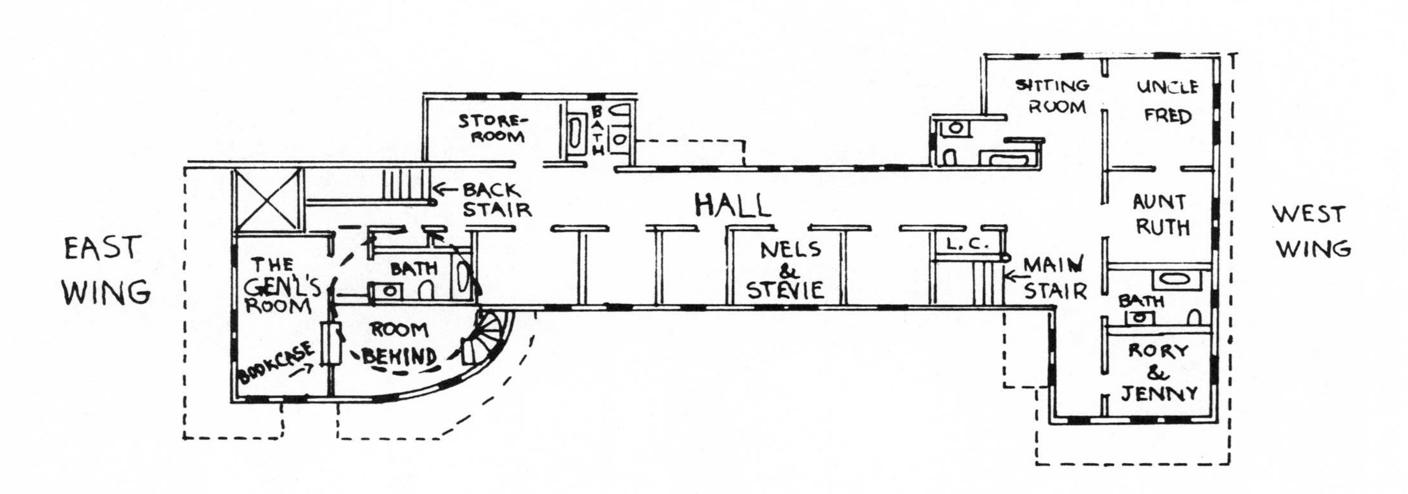
THE INN
SECOND FLOOR
EAST WING
WEST WING
STORE-ROOM
BATH
BACK STAIR
HALL
SITTING ROOM
UNCLE FRED
AUNT RUTH
THE GEN'L'S ROOM
BATH
NELS & STEVIE
L.C.
MAIN STAIR
BATH
ROOM BEHIND
BOOKCASE
RORY & JENNY

I

THE GENERAL'S ROOM

"NELS! Hey, *Nels!*" Stevie was calling, far away downstairs somewhere. "D'you know where Nels is, Rory? . . . Nels! . . . Nels?"

Stevie's voice sounded more distinct suddenly, as if he were heading toward the stairs. Quickly Nels turned away from the door of the big east bedroom—the room he'd never known was there until today. He had been standing as if rooted, staring at that door with its full-length mirror, and wondering if he could possibly have seen what he thought he had seen a few minutes before. *It was a trick of light or something,* he told himself. *My imagination.* Or was it? Heart thumping, he hurried down the dark little passage, slipped into the upstairs hall, and walked rapidly and as quietly as he could back down the long, creaky corridor, past the bedroom he shared with Stevie, past the big linen closet. He managed to reach the newel-post at the head of the main stair just as Stevie's towhead appeared in the gloom of the stairwell.

"Hey, I was calling you. How come you didn't answer?" Hoisting himself by the banister, Stevie took the last three steps to the landing in one, and stood watching as Nels descended to meet him.

"I answered," Nels said as casually as he could. "You just didn't hear me. What do you want?"

"How come I didn't hear you? Where were you?"

"Just—up there." Nels flapped a dismissing hand toward their room, hoping to discourage the flow of questions, wishing he wouldn't keep feeling breathless. "What's the difference where I was?"

"What's wrong?" Stevie's clear blue eyes were studying him in a puzzled, honest way that made Nels want to fly into pieces, or jump out a window or something.

"Nothing's wrong," he said carefully. "Not one single thing. Why don't you tell me what you want?"

After a moment Stevie said, "What I want?"

"You were *calling* me, weren't you?" Nels exploded. "There must have been some reason?"

"Oh." Stevie's eyes were still studying him—a little less bright now, clouded over with the bleak look Nels was beginning to find familiar. "Aunt Ruth rang the bell for lunch."

"Well, why couldn't you just say so?" Nels muttered. He brushed past Stevie and started down the rest of the stairs, thinking, *I didn't need to bite his head off*, then wishing he could quit feeling guilty about every little thing, especially anything to do with Stevie. Wanting to keep just one thing all to yourself wasn't any crime, was it? When you got to be twelve you needed a *tiny* bit of privacy. Brothers could be a drag sometimes—his friend Tom Curtis said the same. Especially brothers two years younger, that you'd sort of outgrown lately. Not the much younger ones, like Rory—and not Jenny, little sisters were okay. But Stevie . . .

Nels's self-defense collapsed. It was Stevie he'd always felt closest to, before. They'd always been a sort of pair, as Rory and Jenny were still. *He* was probably the drag himself. He'd had plenty of hints to that effect from his mother, all through the spring. Always moping. Hard to live with. But who could help it, with everything at home sort of—going to pieces, the way it was? She'd been pretty hard to live with herself. *Nels, please come out of that daydream and help Rory; Nels, you might show some patience, you're the oldest; Nels, please don't be difficult today, I've got to depend on you.* Of course, things were going to pieces for her, too. Had gone to pieces. Nels knew that. But sometimes, these last months, he'd been ready to just take off—run right out the door and keep running till he found some place where he could *think*, could sort of get himself together and find out how he felt about everything. Especially about what Dad had said one day—about teaming up. Whatever he'd meant. Or better still, to *quit* thinking about it.

For a second there, on his way down the stairs, Nels let his mind touch it cautiously again—let himself wonder how it would feel, just Dad and him, living on their own . . . if that was what Dad had meant. No brothers around at all. Or any mother. Or even Jenny. It was impossible to imagine—almost scary. Even trying made him feel so strange and uneasy that he shoved the thought hastily away.

"I wish we were home," Stevie was saying mournfully, following him down the stairs. "I wish Gram was alive so we could go stay at her house, instead of here at old Reeves Ferry."

"Well, she's not. We're stuck with Reeves Ferry. For quite a while." All summer long, Nels thought, suddenly tired to his very bones. Two more months of this dislocated feeling, of a billion questions with no answers, of not knowing exactly what Dad had meant or being able to stop worrying about it. The weariness lifted as he thought of the big bedroom he'd discovered today, with its mirrored door. If only he could have that place to get away to for a while, just now and then . . .

"You don't have to be so crabby," Stevie was mumbling.

"I don't mean to be," Nels said as patiently as he could, resolving once more that he *would* be patient with Stevie. Besides, something was warning him urgently to get hold of himself and act normal—show neither impatience nor secret excitement. Nobody must know about that room just yet—or what he'd seen in the mirror. If he'd really seen anything. He must get back soon and find out. Right after lunch—

"Hey, you want to ride bikes after lunch?" Stevie asked as they headed for the dining room.

"No," Nels said. To head off the inevitable "Why not?" he swerved suddenly toward the little bathroom across from the foot of the stairs, adding, "Come on, let's wash our hands. Aunt Ruth's sure to ask us."

"Gol, you never want to do anything any more," complained Stevie as he followed.

"I just don't want to go bike riding, that's all. Why can't you go by yourself?"

"I'm not supposed to go farther than the schoolyard unless you're with me. And those big guys are always hanging around there. Anyway, it's no fun alone. Gol."

"Don't say 'gol', it sounds dumb. I'll go with you some other time. I want to read, after lunch."

"Gol, all you ever want to do is read! How about let's play Snap or something? Rummy?"

"I said I want to *read*." Nels snatched the towel away from him. "You didn't use soap."

"Aw, shut up, you're as bad as Mommie!" yelled Stevie, then fell abruptly silent, turned away, and began to soap his hands.

Nels hung up the towel and walked quickly out of the room and down the main hall toward the dining room, wishing the same silly quarrels wouldn't keep happening over and over and everybody, including himself, wouldn't keep making the same dumb mistakes with one another. His surroundings did nothing to cheer him. The downstairs hall was wider than the one upstairs, but just as long and creaky, and almost as gloomy. Some of the old hotel lobby armchairs, looking out-of-date and sad, stood here and there along it like driftwood left by the tide, and on the wall above them hung clusters of dim and faded photographs.

Stevie caught up as he passed the big front door, saying in a conciliatory tone, "Well, after you get through reading, maybe we could play chess."

"You don't know how to play chess, that I ever heard of."

"You could teach me, couldn't you? Same as Daddy taught you. *He's* not going to be around to teach me," Stevie added, half under his breath.

"You don't know that," Nels said sternly. Stevie was breaking an unspoken rule. They never discussed the divorce, the four of them, even among themselves. For all Nels knew, Rory and Jenny didn't even grasp what this summer was all about, and what was going on, back in Portland, while they put in the boring, lonely days here at Reeves Ferry, with nothing to do, no friends, no library, no swimming class, no Ruffles to throw sticks for, no parents—not even yelling, fighting parents. Maybe never two parents again. Only which one . . . ? How . . . ? Who was going to *decide*?

Nels forced the panic rush of questions back into the darkest closet of his mind and slammed the door. "I'll play checkers with you," he said rapidly. "*One* game. Right after lunch. If you'll leave me alone, then."

"Okay. I will, honest," Stevie said. "I don't mind checkers. I even sort of like them," he added firmly.

And after *that* I'll go back upstairs to the east room, Nels thought, and find out what I saw.

They went through the tall, narrow opening framed by the sliding doors, into the dining room, and around one side of the big oval table to stand behind their chairs, awaiting the daily noontime ritual of the meal.

ALMOST EVERYTHING was a ritual at Uncle Fred and Aunt Ruth Webster's house—or the Inn, as everybody around Reeves Ferry still called it. These days it was a strange old rambling building, with one wing turned into Websters' Grocery (run by their great-aunt and uncle), another chunk rented to a realty company, some rooms lived in, and some left empty. But it really had been an inn to begin with. Alice Clary, who was the housekeeper and cook—and as it worked out, chief boss of the Anderson children too—had told the four of them all about it on their first afternoon there, nearly three weeks ago.

It was a bad afternoon, that first one, strange and lonesome. They'd spent half the day driving the two hundred fifty miles from the city in Dad's noisy old Chevy, crammed in with their luggage and their forebodings, with nobody in the mood to talk. Then they'd followed Dad into the Inn and upstairs, suitcases banging their legs, and dumped their familiar belongings in the two strange new rooms. For a while they'd stood around in a silent cluster as Dad and Aunt Ruth made hearty conversation, both saying a lot of things twice. Then Aunt Ruth had to hurry back to her grocery customers, and Dad had to say good-bye. And Nels, Stevie, Rory and Jenny had to stand watching him drive away toward the freeway to start the other hundred miles to Millerton and the new, unknown place he lived.

That was the worst part by far, but Alice cut it short by ordering them all inside to unpack their clothes and stow away their suitcases and wash their hands with soap and come down to her kitchen when they'd finished. By that time they were beginning to want to know something about this real weird place they were in, and Alice was ready to tell them. The Inn at Reeves Ferry, she informed them, had once been a fashionable resort hotel. City people used to flock here, to boat on the river and picnic along its banks; expert swimmers could even go in—though the Anderson children could *not*. And there'd once been a huge lounge (now the store), a billiard room (now the stock room) and a fine rose garden out back. But the old days were gone; there hadn't been a paying guest here since before even Nels was born—except for old General Rutherford, who'd rented the big east bedroom till he died.

"And now there's *you*," Alice had added, with her pert, twisted little smile that Nels couldn't decide whether to accept as friendly or not. "You're paying guests. Aren't you?"

She happened to be looking at Stevie, so he said, "I don't know," and looked at Nels, who didn't know either, but said, "We're relatives. Uncle Fred is our mother's uncle."

"Oh, I know all about that," Alice retorted. She was counting out silverware in the narrow, high-ceilinged butler's pantry between the kitchen and the huge dining room. "But your keep's being paid for, just the same. So I understand. Even these two teddy bears," She reached down a long forefinger to push Rory's nose, then Jenny's, as if she were ringing doorbells. Rory and Jenny just stared at her, with their heads, one blond, one tawny, tilted back at identical angles. "I've got a teddy bear of my own," she told them, still in that tone that made you expect her to add, *So there!* "Just about your age. How old are you?"

"Eight," said Rory.

"I'm six," said Jenny.

"Well, my Maureen is seven, so you'll likely turn right into the Gleesome Threesome. I'll bring her over tomorrow and see if it works, okay? Get the whole batch of you out from underfoot."

"Okay," said Jenny and Rory expressionlessly.

They didn't know how to take her, Nels could tell. He didn't, himself. She was a lanky, angular woman, slightly older than their own mother, with an unexpected litheness when she was moving, and an unexpected snub nose in an otherwise longish, horsey sort of face. And she kept unexpectedly saying friendly things in an unfriendly way—or mixing friendly things with sudden little jibes. Rory and Jenny evidently decided she meant they were underfoot now, and took themselves off somewhere, but Nels hung around, and followed Alice when she carried her tray of silverware into the dining room. Stevie dawdled after him.

"Shall I help you set the table?" Nels asked formally.

"You'd best just watch a few times till you get onto our little ways here. They're not like your ways or my ways, maybe, but they're the Inn's ways. We're most particular, we are."

Nels drifted over toward the windows—there were six of them in a long, curved bay that formed one wall—and watched her arrange silver on the oval table. It was a large table, but in that hotel-sized room, under that high, shadowed ceiling, it had a frail and temporary look on its patch of carpet. The light was pallid, filtered through thin curtains and dimmed by the huge fir tree outside. Scarcely a gleam reached all the way across to touch the dark wainscoting of the opposite wall, where there was a vast, built-in sideboard—banks of drawers and a service counter, empty cupboards with beveled glass doors—none of it used now, that Nels could see.

"What's all that for?" asked Stevie. He was staring at the sideboard too.

"For all us waitresses, that's what," Alice told him. "In the old days when this place was the Inn, we kept the glassware in those cupboards, and napkins in those drawers—real cloth napkins, mind you, starched to a board, none of your cheesy paper things—and our little silver coffee pots there on the shelf. Used to be ten tables in this room! And five of us waitresses. Kids—fresh out of high school. We wore yellow dresses and aprons with big bows behind—like a bunch of butterflies swarming around in here. Can't you see us?" She gave a conjurer's airy wave and Nels *could* see them suddenly, ghostly butterfly figures (one angular and snub-nosed) fluttering about with silver coffee pots among the chattering guests.

The cheerful vision faded. "Ten tables like that one?" Nels asked, trying to summon it back.

"No, no. The rest were smaller. That Fisherman's Lodge place—up by Easterside—they bought 'em. The big one's just a leftover. Same as the sideboard. Same as me. We're all leftovers in this house, don't you know that?" She gave him her twisty smile, hands deft and quick among the forks and spoons.

Nels glanced at her sharply, then away. For a second it seemed a deliberate flick on the raw—as if she had taken one look at the four of them and come up with the perfect description. Leftovers! It was how they had all been feeling. *Forget it*, Nels ordered himself, avoiding Stevie's eye. She was only talking about herself—and maybe Aunt Ruth and Uncle Fred.

Stevie had turned his back, produced one of his miniature racing cars from his pocket and was running it along the windowsills, leaping it gracefully from one to the other and *vroom-vrooming* under his breath. Maybe he hadn't noticed the crack about leftovers—if it was a crack. Wishing miserably that he hadn't noticed it either, Nels got his mind off it with an effort and back on the ghosts of breakfasts past. "How come it stopped being a real inn?" he asked. The old days sounded much livelier.

"They put in the freeway, and Easterside Bridge," Alice said. "They got all these motels around there now. Reeves Ferry's just a dead end. Ferryboat's chopped up for kindling, for all I know. And the old Inn's nothing—just that big old barn next to the store, where the Websters live."

"Next to the store? It *is* the store, isn't it?" Stevie turned to stare at her. "I mean the store's right in this building. Right down there." He pointed out the window, where beyond the big fir and some scraggly shrubs and a stretch of weed-grown flagstones and lawn going bald, the Inn's west wing thrust out to face the dining room where they stood. It made a big E, this building—Nels realized it as if he were suddenly high above it looking down. The front walk—those flagstones—formed the middle stroke between the two thrust-out wings.

Alice gave her short little laugh. "Sure, the Inn's the store, if your mind's on a peck of potatoes and some toothpaste. The tail's the dog, if you're a flea." She tucked her empty tray under her arm and grinned at Stevie. "Mr. Big-Eyes."

Stevie's eyes had certainly opened to their widest—with blank surprise turning to resentment. He had never been able to understand teasing, well-intentioned or otherwise, and now he clearly felt he was being insulted. "I'm not a flea," he said. "Or a Mr. Big-Eyes either. *Or* a leftover," he muttered to Nels.

"Oh, she didn't mean anything," Nels said under his breath. "Don't be so literal."

Stevie gave him a *don't you start* glance. He heard quite enough about "literal" from their mother, Nels knew—as much as Nels himself heard about "woolgathering" and "day-dreaming." But before he could add anything, Stevie had turned away, saying, "Come on, let's go outdoors."

"You wouldn't go off mad?" Alice was half-cajoling, now. But Stevie kept going, head averted, all his attention apparently on stuffing the racing car back into his pocket.

Nels hung around a moment longer, then followed at a stroll.

He didn't object to Alice, he decided, though he couldn't make her out. But she'd lost Stevie for good; he'd probably never like her now. Stevie was that way.

BY THIS TIME, nearly three dragging weeks later, Nels had begun to wish heartily that Stevie was not that way, or that Alice had put her foot right with him instead of wrong. In avoiding her, Stevie had also dealt himself right out of the games and pastimes she thought up to occupy the younger ones—Rory and Jenny and fat little Maureen. They had become a threesome just as Alice had predicted, with Rory leader of the parade. That left Stevie turning more and more persistently to Nels—for companionship, for everything—until he felt like a hundred-pound millstone around Nels's neck.

And a restless, fidgeting sort of millstone he was right now, as they waited at their places for lunch—leaning first one elbow then the other on the back of his chair until the chair tipped, then, as he caught it, joggling the precisely set table.

"Watch *out*," Nels implored, restoring the nearest silverware to its rigid order.

"Well, where are they? Why do we always have to stand around?"

"She has to bring him from the store. You know that."

"So why doesn't she bring him before we come, then?"

Nels didn't answer. Stevie knew as well as he that it was just one of the rituals, one of their "little ways" here at the Inn. Like the table setting—each spoon laid crosswise above the plate, each napkin folded into a stiff-starched crown on the plate, each knife blade resting on a strange little stand like a tiny silver sawhorse.

The chatter and laughing from the kitchen grew louder, then ceased as the pantry doors swung open to admit Rory and Jenny marching to their chairs like soldiers, elbows stiff, chins high, clowning as usual, and as usual convulsing each other. Maureen's voice piped something from the kitchen and produced falling-around giggles in the two younger Andersons.

"*Gol*. You guys are so dumb," Stevie told them disgustedly.

"Dumb! We're *dumb*. Help, help, I've lost me voice . . ." Rory clutched his throat and mouthed distractedly, sending Jenny into a fresh burst of hilarity and an attempt at imitation.

Nels shushed them both, but smiled in spite of himself because Rory really was comical, and Jenny—with her hoarse little voice and kitten's face and tawny silk hair—well, Jenny was just Jenny; whatever she did seemed okay to Nels. "Be quiet," he said. "They're coming."

The footsteps were finally creaking their slow way along the hall; a pause by the main entrance, the two voices murmuring—one solicitous, questioning, the other a brief rumble—then the creaking again, the soft drag of the slipper, and at last Uncle Fred appeared in the doorway, leaning heavily on his cane and on Aunt Ruth's arm—a big, drooping hawk supported by a sparrow. She gave a quick, absent smile around the table as she piloted him across the last stretch of bare floor.

"Well, here you all are—and are your hands nice and clean? Used the soap, did you? Hung the towel up?" There was a ragged chorus of assent, but she was already checking the table setting, the level of the blinds at the windows, the presence of Uncle Fred's two pill bottles on the sideboard, one more beside his plate. He was cautiously lowering himself into the big host's chair. "Well, let's all sit down," she went on as he subsided with a final grunt. She moved to the chair beside him, calling,

"All right, Alice!" And instantaneously there was Alice coming through the swinging door with the big tray of soup plates, like a genie from a bottle. Nels had decided she must wait just behind it, the laden tray in her hands, while they were all waiting behind their chairs. He picked up his spoon, resigned to the obligatory three mouthfuls, though he hated soup.

The next part of the ritual came very shortly; the throat-clearing sigh from Uncle Fred, the slow pushing back of his soup plate, the easing of his grizzled head against the high chair back, the vague, benevolent smile around the table. "Well, children? . . . Had a pleasant morning, did you? . . . Didn't get into mischief?"

They muttered yeses and noes.

"That's fine, fine . . . yes. Nice bunch of kids . . . Very nice . . . Glad to have you here."

"Fred, can't you eat just a little more of your soup?" Aunt Ruth asked him.

"No, no. I've had a-plenty."

"Alice!" called Aunt Ruth.

Next came the slow, painful turning of the uncle's head and once-powerful shoulders (toward Stevie today), the hint of banter creeping into the rumbling voice and a faint twinkle appearing under the thatch of eyebrow. "Well, young man? What have you to say for yourself today?"

And Stevie's bashful, "Nothing," and a half-grin; he'd taken a liking to Uncle Fred from the beginning, with as little reason as he'd had for his dislike of Alice.

"So—what's nine times nine, hey? . . . Can you tell me that?"

Stevie might have paused for thought two and a half weeks ago when they arrived here, but he didn't now. If nothing else came of this miserable summer, Nels reflected, at least all of them knew beyond doubt that nine times nine was eighty-one.

Also that Columbia was the capital of South Carolina (his own ritual lunchtime question), that "receive" was spelled "e-i" (Rory's) and that Jenny did indeed have a doll and its name was Ann Anderson. Uncle Fred never forgot whose turn it was to be asked a question, but he either couldn't or didn't bother to remember any of their names, simply calling them all "young man" ("young lady" in Jenny's case) and letting it go at that.

By now he was murmuring his usual "very good, yes, good," to Stevie's sheepish but smiling response, and Aunt Ruth was handing his water glass, saying, "Your yellow pill, Fred," and that ritual was over for the day. Alice began whisking away soup bowls and replacing them with lunch (chicken, potatoes, carrots, apple salad—dinner, it would have been at home; but here they had the lunchy things like peanut butter sandwiches at night) and Nels was free to unleash his thoughts from the here and now. Immediately they flew upstairs, and back to that strange half-hour before lunch.

AT ELEVEN-THIRTY he had been wandering alone down the long upstairs hall, walking east toward the unoccupied reaches of the second floor—just poking about aimlessly because anything was better than sitting alone, thinking. Stevie and Rory had left right after breakfast to start some bridge-building project, and perversely, the minute he was free of Stevie, Nels longed for his company. He'd finished the book he'd been reading. Alice was busy vacuuming. There was nothing to do.

And he couldn't bear another minute of thinking about

yesterday's letter from his mother. Last Friday, she'd managed to come to see them. It was the Fourth of July and for once she had two consecutive days off from her new job at the dress shop. She'd spent a great part of them in a Greyhound bus, making the five hundred mile round trip for a visit with her children. And it hadn't worked. None of them could enjoy it for dreading the moment it must end. And the end was awful—Jenny clinging and screaming, their mother in tears, the others desperate for her to leave and get it over with. They were all tired and cross-grained the whole next day. It had been almost a relief yesterday when letters came from her—one for each child—explaining that she would not come down again. Nels's letter had said, "I'm counting on you to help the little ones understand. Dear old Nels, you just don't *know* how much I'll be counting on you for the next few years . . ."

The bare thought of that letter was enough to start the unanswerable questions roiling about again in the dark waters of his mind, first one then another bobbing to the surface like spawning monsters, and having to be pushed under again quickly before you could see their scarey, half-formed faces. When that began, even exploring the unoccupied areas of the Inn's second floor was a welcome diversion.

Not that there seemed much of interest to discover. Just a long wasteland of hall with a threadbare runner of carpet, a dim, high ceiling, stray cobwebs, creakings that seemed to have no connection with Nels's quiet movements. Along the hall to his left, beyond the room he shared with Stevie, there was only a row of closed doors, shutting off disused bedrooms and service closets, as he found by peeking in. On the right, several tall, narrow windows, too heavily draped to admit much light, offered glimpses of the derelict rose garden behind the Inn. Between the windows hung more groupings of faded framed photographs—one was of a senator-looking man in a flat straw hat posed in front of the main entrance, another showed a man and woman standing beside a car, and a boy perched on its folded-back top waving at the camera. The car had a fancy radiator cap and wire wheels—were they in the 'Twenties or 'Thirties? Tom Curtis would have known. Tom could have told exactly what kind of car it was, and maybe what model. For that matter, Tom could have thought up something better to do than stare at old photographs. He'd have thought of a dozen things by now, all of them interesting. Everything would be interesting if only Tom were here—if *some* friend of his own age and tastes were here.

Nels turned hastily and walked on, opened and closed two doors on the right beyond the windows, (a storeroom, and a high-ceiling, white-tiled bathroom, cozy as an abandoned refrigerator, with empty grocery cartons piled in the tub) and then found himself peering down a narrow stair that apparently led to the kitchen passage and back door.

The long west-east hall ended there, beside the stair, in a shallow alcove containing a table with nothing on it. Slightly puzzled, Nels peered through the shadows to his left, scanning the dark-paneled wall. It should open out here into the east wing—that bottom stroke of the E which right-angled sharply toward the road. Surely there were rooms above the dining room and kitchen? Then there ought to be a transverse hall right here, or at least another of those tight-shut bedroom doors that were the reason this corner was so dark you mightn't see an elephant unless you fell over it! *Was* that a door?—no, just a carved section of the paneling, Nels decided, walking over to it. Or rather, a sort of—screen. Not the folding kind, but a free-standing panel of age-black wood, heavily carved and pierced, like clumsy lace. He squinted through one of the meagre openings, then triumphantly squeezed around one side of the screen and behind it into the east wing hall he sought.

At first it scarcely seemed worth the trouble. The passage was murky and narrow, unexpectedly short, and filled entirely at the far end by a huge piece of furniture. something ornate with drawers, barely visible in the gloom. A door at his left hand disclosed a bathroom with one small, dim lamp and crimson-striped wallpaper that made Nels dizzy just peeking in. A few steps ahead on the right, a streak of daylight fell across the worn carpet from another door, half-open into a surprisingly large, bright room—very likely that "big east bedroom" Alice had said the old General rented till he died. Suddenly feeling like an intruder, Nels only glanced through the doorway and was about to turn away when something caught his eye.

The door had a full-length mirror on its outer side. And the mirror reflected an image. It was a boy about Nels's age—a total stranger.

The image was gone so quickly that at once Nels doubted he'd really seen it. According to Alice, nobody lived in this room now. Nobody had for years. He wasted a precious moment staring stupidly at the mirror, now reflecting a patch of wall and half a dresser. Then he stepped forward, into the doorway, and looked directly at the whole dresser, the whole side wall, the east windows straight in front of him. No sign of occupancy, or any boy. Cautiously, ready for swift retreat, he took a soundless step inside and peered around the door.

The room was empty.

It was far longer than the passage, extending clear to the front of the house. He stood rock-still while his eyes investigated every object, every inch. A blue rug, a quilt-covered bed, two chairs—one hard, one soft. Between the two front windows, a desk, bare except for a pad of yellow paper. Three windows with thin curtains in the east wall opposite the door. Behind the half-open door and in the same west wall, a built-in bookcase. No second way out.

Then what had he seen? A shadow, he told himself. Some trick of light. Maybe you saw yourself, reflected back somehow from that dresser mirror or a window pane, or . . .

But hadn't he got a clear impression of *dark* hair?

No. He'd got no *clear* impression of anything—except a boy shape. What you got, he told himself, was a sort of mental snapshot of Tom Curtis. You got a clear impression of wishful thinking, *that's* what you got. Remember the time you *knew* you saw Dad sitting in the living room window—and he was in Coos Bay? Remember the kitten you *knew* you heard in the linen cupboard, that summer you wanted a kitten so bad? Okay, then. Forget it.

He could not forget it. He began to walk around the room, instead. It was a fine room—large and light and pleasant, if a trifle bare. And really private. It would be a wonderful place to come—just for an hour sometimes—a place to keep for himself alone.

Well, I suppose I'd tell Stevie, Nels thought guiltily. Though Stevie wouldn't really care much for it. Poking around indoors and finding nice secret places wasn't his sort of thing at all. Stevie liked the open; he liked to go outside. I could keep it secret for a while, Nels told himself. Until Stevie asked . . . But why should he ask? What if I never did tell him—or anybody—just this once? Nobody would dream of looking for me in this room. Nobody else even knows it's here! Except Aunt Ruth and Uncle Fred, of course, and probably Alice—and *they* don't know *I* know. And if I was careful, and never let myself be seen . . .

Nels glanced at the bedroom door, the one with the mirror. Surely he'd seen a dark-haired boy. Wearing something *red*. He glanced down at his own shirt: a pale, checked blue. His heart began a slow, deep thudding that disturbed his breathing.

He was still standing there when he'd heard Stevie calling him to lunch.

"... THE HONEY, Nels?" Rory was asking. "Neh-yuls. Hey, Nellie!"

"Don't call me Nellie!" Nels commanded, coming out of his preoccupation with a rush and back to the lunch table.

"Only thing that'll wake ya' up," Rory said airily. He was extending the honey dish at a wobbling forty-five degree angle, elbow on table. "D'you want this or don't you?"

"No, thank you, and watch out!" Nels rescued the dish and set it down, then with a glance at his plate, put his fork down, too. Who could eat all that stuff at *lunchtime*? Except Stevie, who could eat any amount at any time, though he stayed rail-thin. He was actually buttering a second roll. Even Jenny was still busy with a drumstick. They were all still eating. Lunch would never be over.

There couldn't have been any boy in that mirror, Nels thought. I only saw some freak reflection of myself . . . But it was odd he should keep feeling he'd seen dark hair. Darker than Jenny's—hers was reddish, like a hazelnut. This had been almost black. And his own was about the color of that honey. So where did that leave the freak-reflection theory? And he was almost sure he'd seen something red.

You're not really sure of anything, said a chilly little voice inside him. But a louder one whispered, *shut up*.

Nels roused himself, passed the butter Aunt Ruth was asking

for, and finding his mouth oddly dry, finished his milk. He was feeling breathless again—he wondered if it showed. The only thing to do was to go back to that mirror and look again—then he'd *know.* Right after lunch. That is, right after the checker game he'd promised Stevie.

Stevie was talking to Uncle Fred now, telling him shyly about teaching Ruffles to sit up, and what Ruffles looked like and how near Ruffles was to being an almost purebred dog, though *not* a spitz as people always thought—while Uncle Fred smiled amiably if absent-mindedly and gave an occasional nod. *He's not really listening*, Nels thought, feeling a prickle of mortification for Stevie's sake.

"Can't you eat more of that chicken, Fred?" Aunt Ruth cut in, right across Stevie's voice as if he hadn't been saying a word.

"No, no, I've had a-plenty, my dear. Very tasty lunch."

"Well, anyway," Stevie struggled on, "anyway, we think her father was a white collie—"

"But, my conscience, you've hardly eaten a thing! I declare, I don't know what to tell Alice to fix—"

"Now, Ruth, there's not a thing wrong with the food. I don't require much, that's all."

Stevie, waiting with mouth ajar, glanced at Aunt Ruth, and when she merely sighed, took up his narrative. "—and the mother was a *full-blood* fox terrier. So she's lots prettier than a spitz. And the reason we named her—"

"Well, take your other pill, then. Did you take it already?"

"I took all three."

"Uncle Fred?—the reason we named her Ruffles—"

"Stevie *dear*!" said Aunt Ruth. "Can't you see I'm speaking to your uncle? You mustn't interrupt like that."

"Now, Ruth, I've had a fine lunch and a packet of horsepills. Nothing wrong with me but meanness. And this young man was telling me all about his spitz puppy. Pretty dogs, spitzes.

What's his name again, Old Timer? Go right ahead with what you were going to say."

Stevie looked at him silently a moment, then muttered, "Oh—it wasn't anything . . ."

"Everybody ready for ice cream, then?" said Aunt Ruth briskly. "Alice?"

Nels turned away before Stevie had a chance to seek his eye. *He* couldn't help things like this happening, he told himself quickly. Stevie let himself in for them. Stevie wasn't *his* lookout—not to that extent. He hated this summer himself, he had enough on his mind already. Anyhow, he'd promised to play checkers, hadn't he? He supposed he'd better teach Stevie chess, too, while he had a chance. Because maybe after September he and Dad both . . .

Nels trod hard on his thoughts and switched them by force to the dessert Alice was bringing in. "Hey, Jenny," he said abruptly, leaning forward to peer around Rory. "Which are you going to have on your ice cream today, chocolate sauce or jam?"

Jenny grinned sidewise at him, not bothering to answer. "Pigwidgeon," their Dad used to call her—that was some kind of imp-creature only Dad had ever heard of, that he said lived on chocolate sauce and fudge. Jenny's wide mouth, a long pink curve curled up at the corners, was smeary from the drumstick, and her napkin, of course, nowhere in sight. Nels found it for her, reaching across Rory to do so and welcoming the commotion created by Rory's theatrical self-effacing and apologies for living, since it kept his mind off anything else. But at last dessert was finished, and they were free. The younger two rushed straight through the swinging pantry door to the kitchen and Maureen; Nels and Stevie went back to the main hall and along to the big bay window between the dining room and the front door. A game table nearly filled the deep, three-sided alcove.

"Gol, it takes hours and hours around here just to eat lunch!" Stevie muttered as they arrived.

"I *know*," Nels agreed with feeling.

"Not that there's anything else to do." Stevie rummaged in the cupboards under the curving window seat, found the checkers box and board, and slung them onto the table. "Gol, I sure wish we could've brought Ruffles," he added.

"Uncle Fred is too sick to have a dog around. Besides—"

"I know, I know, I was only wishing. I can wish, can't I? I want the red ones, okay?" Stevie began arranging his side of the board, placing each disk precisely in the center of its square. "What's the matter with him, anyhow?"

"Uncle Fred? I don't know, isn't it his heart or something?" Nels tried to remember what his mother had said about it—if anything—then gave it up and shrugged.

"Maybe he had a stroke," Stevie said. "What's a stroke?"

"*I* don't know. I get to move first this time."

"It must hurt him a lot," Stevie said. "He takes an awful lot of pills."

"That doesn't mean it hurts him a lot. Maybe the pills keep it *from* hurting him."

"He looks like it hurts him a lot," Stevie said. "I wish we had a basketball hoop here. That wouldn't bother him, would it? I wish we could go in the river! At home, I'd be starting that swimming class next week. Gol, now it'll be another whole year before I learn! I bet I don't get to take it then, either. Last summer I had chicken pox, and this summer I'm at dumb old Reeves Ferry, and probably next summer—"

"*Move*. Do you want to play this game or not?"

Stevie moved, sighed, gazed drearily out the window. After a moment he said, "Hey, Nels? D'you think we'll still live on Forty-fifth Street after . . . you know."

Nels knew. After the divorce. Or whatever was going to

happen. He wasn't really sure what else might happen—what the alternatives were, if any. His mother would not discuss it. "Nels, I can't give you answers. I've got to take one thing at a time—one day at a time. For the spring, I've got this job at the dress shop, and thank heaven, you to babysit after school. When summer comes—well, I'll think of something." What she had thought of was the Inn, and her uncle and aunt who would take four children as paying guests. But there were no plans for September . . . except maybe Dad's. Nels didn't quite know what those were. And he didn't want to talk about it.

"I don't know where we'll live," he told Stevie.

"Gol, I hope we don't have to change schools again! Anyway, I like it where we live. With the Curtises right across the street and all. Graham's going to show me how to make one of those overpasses for my train layout. He was going to do it this summer," Stevie added disconsolately. "Right about now."

"I wish you'd quit moaning and groaning, and play, if you're going to. I jumped your man—look."

Stevie looked, turned back to the board, and jumped one of Nels's. For a while they played in silence. But Nels, now, was having trouble keeping his mind on the game. Stevie's mention of Graham Curtis had reminded him that Tom had got a hand printing press for his birthday, late in May. They'd barely got started on what they'd expected would fill their summer—putting out a neighborhood newspaper, *The Daily Blah*. It would've been so great, Nels thought with longing. They'd succeeded in printing one issue, a dozen or so copies, after nearly a week of fooling with the press, learning to handle the rubber type, and figuring out what they were supposed to do—because of course the instructions had got lost right away. Then it had turned out they were mixing up "p's" with "b's" and "d's" and "q's" and their first issue had been so full of crazy mistakes they'd nearly died laughing, looking at it.

Nels was half-smiling, just remembering, until Stevie said, "Hey, king me!" in an astonished voice, and he realized he was going to lose the game if he didn't pay attention. Not that it mattered. The sooner somebody lost, the sooner he'd be free to go back upstairs. Still . . . he couldn't lose, he was supposed to be the family expert. He'd always won those checkers tournaments they used to have, back when they lived on Oriole Street. That was ages ago, when Jenny was just a baby. They used to do a lot of things together then, all of them, Dad *and* Mom, and Stevie and Rory and him. And he couldn't remember anybody being snappish or cross—at least, only normally, not like . . . A picture formed in his mind, of the downstairs of the Forty-fifth Street house the way it looked last spring, after the couch got the hole burnt in it and Rory'd spilled that ink on the hall rug, with the usual soundtrack of arguing and fighting, angry voices behind a closed bedroom door, ending sometimes with a final bellow from his father, sometimes with just a slammed door and silence, then his mother crying—and he felt the familiar sort of sick, heavy sensation, as if he were drowning.

"I won!" cried Stevie.

Nels came to with a shock to focus stupidly on the board. It was true. He blinked at Stevie, whose face was alight.

"Gol, I *never* won before! Especially from you! Hey, want to play best two out of three?"

"No," Nels said quickly. He stood up, reached for the box that held the checkers.

"Aw, come on! Just because you can't win every time—!"

"It's not that! I said I'd play one game. Well, I did. Help me put them away—there's one on the floor over there."

"Aw, *gol* . . ." Stevie dived for the piece, came up flushed and sulky.

They put away the game in silence, moved from the table. Nels dawdled, willing Stevie to go, go, get out of sight. "Weren't you and Rory going to finish that bridge?" he said.

"Yeah. But he's probably gone by now. Over to Maureen's."

"Well, you can find him." For another moment Nels clung by main force to his wooden expression of unconcern, then he *had* to edge away. Awkwardly, he said, "Well, so long. See you later."

"Yeah." Stevie thrust his hands into his pockets, glanced at Nels. The light was gone from his face, the bleak look back. He wandered off across the hall toward the Rooftop Realty Company—once the old Inn office—and turned down the back passage, while Nels watched and fought down the impulse to call him back, play one more game. *But I can't, I'll get thinking again*, cried something desperate inside him. *It's okay, he'll find Rory* . . . But Stevie didn't want to find Rory, Nels had seen that. Stevie was outgrowing Rory and turning to *him*, just as he was outgrowing Stevie and turning . . . Where?

He flung his thoughts away from him, trampled them underfoot as he fled furiously up the stairs.

ARRIVING BREATHLESS at the top, he listened until he was sure nobody was on the second floor but him. Then he hurried on down the long hall to the other end. He hesitated, peering warily down the service stairs. He was now just above where Stevie had vanished, and he hadn't yet heard the back door slam—but no matter. Maybe this once Stevie had closed it gently. Nels turned, slid behind the carved screen into the east wing passage, and moved swiftly toward the big room.

The door was still half-open. He paused, heart thudding again, then made himself relax and step forward in an ordinary, casual way. As he did so, the floor creaked under him.

And from the room he caught a fainter sound—swift, stealthy, gone before he could identify it or even be sure he had heard it. The mirror was empty.

He caught his breath, ran forward into the room. It, too, was empty, unchanged since he'd left it. He found himself standing beside the east windows, looking down on a strip of flat roof edged with pointy iron railing and covered with buckling composition, stuff that glittered faintly here and there. Below, aimlessly crossing the driveway with his hands in his pockets, was Stevie—the only person in sight.

So sick with disappointment that he was surprised at himself, Nels turned back into the room. Surely he had heard something! A swift sound of movement—and the faintest of clicks, like a . . . like a latch closing.

A latch closing. At once everything was prosaically clear. The sound had not even come from this room but from outdoors. He had merely heard Stevie latch the back gate. Must have. There was nothing to latch in here. Despondently Nels stared around at the sparse furnishings, the two or three dim, high pictures, the faded wallpaper unbroken except by that built-in bookcase. No cupboards, not even a closet door . . . And that was odd. His glance went back to the bookcase. It was the *width* of a closet door. About the shape of one, too, when you thought about it—though taller, extending almost to the ceiling. Nels walked toward it, his attention sharpening. It was not so much built in as built against the wall, like a shallow box with shelves, just tacked up there. In fact, the bottom shelf cleared the floor by an inch or two. Nels pondered that for a minute. Then he was on his knees, peering into the slit of space underneath.

Nothing. A dust mouse that stirred faintly in the dimness as his breathing touched it. Reluctantly, he straightened, then frowned and bent down again, shading his eyes from the window light as he squinted first right, then left. There was one—only one—supporting leg for the front edge of the bookcase: a plain little copper cylinder under the left hand corner, with a flat square base screwed to the floor. Nels reached out a hand to explore the underside of the frame and found more metal; a sort of bracket support extending a good twelve inches from the leg toward the middle, under the bottom shelf.

Something ran tickling across his hand; he jerked it away, shook off a spider, and stood up, backing away from the bookcase for a different sort of scrutiny. Why would anyone put a single cylinder leg under just one corner of a bookcase? For a pivot to turn in, that was why. There must be a matching device on top, where he couldn't see it. The bookcase was a door, which worked on pivots instead of hinges. And the *click* he had heard was the sound of its quiet closing. Nels was ready to bet on it.

If it had closed, it would open. Briefly, Nels tried simple tugging, but was not surprised when nothing happened. It was bound to have a hidden catch of some sort, a secret spring—a fake panel behind the books—even a fake book. Eagerly he began taking books out and stacking them on the floor.

The shelves were not full; the top one held only a defunct clock, and on the others books were grouped, supported by various objects—a brass shell casing, a paperweight like the Eiffel Tower, a thick restaurant mug holding a few pencils and ballpoint pens. Everything was dusty; obviously Alice didn't trouble herself with this part of the house more than once or twice a year.

As he cleared the books off, Nels examined each shelf, running his fingers around the sides, pressing here and there at the back. Nothing. Ten minutes later he stood amidst a clutter looking at an empty and perfectly innocent bookcase. But there was *something*, there had to be. This bookcase was a door, and it concealed something—the entrance to something. On a sudden thought Nels knocked gently on the panel backing the shelves. It did sound hollow. He knocked again—beat a frustrated tattoo, heedless of caution now.

The knocking continued, faintly, an instant after he had stopped. Or was it an echo?

He banged both fists against the panel, cried, "Who are you? If somebody's there, come out! You'll smother to death!" Teeth clenched, skin prickling from sweat and dust and exasperation, he gave the frame one last infuriated shove and turned away in defeat.

Then, soft but distinct, he heard a click. He whirled back, stared with wildly beating heart as the bookcase shuddered slowly outward, like a door, and bumped to a stop against a stack of books.

At the same moment there was a muffled but unquestionably real sound from somewhere under his feet: the familiar whine-screech of the oven door closing, and Alice's voice calling, "What say? Which of you kids was that? I'm in the kitchen!"

Nels froze, suddenly blind to the bookcase he was staring at, as his dismayed attention switched wholly to the sounds below. He could hear Alice's footsteps cross the kitchen accompanied by grumbles, and presently he heard the faint creak of the back screen and her voice, farther away and coming from outside now, calling, "Kids? Maureen?" Then after a pause, more grumbles as she came back to the kitchen.

It was all right—she thought it was somebody outside she'd heard. Nels could almost feel his ears relax, like Ruffles's after a moment of strained listening.

He swallowed, drew a long breath, and with renewed caution stole close enough to move the stack of books out of the way, quickly retreating as the bookcase-door continued its ponderous outward swing until it stopped of itself, about a quarter open. Nothing else happened. No boy appeared.

He took hold of the edge of the bookcase and gently pulled. It was solid, heavier than ordinary doors because of the weight of shelves. Behind it was a dark place. A closet, he saw when he moved out of his own light and pushed the door farther open. He peered into the shadows, but it looked empty: bare board floor, smudged dim walls, an old yardstick with one broken end leaning in a corner. Just a closet, after all.

But what a really weird way to build a closet, especially in an inn! Why, the hotel guests given this room wouldn't have had any place to hang their clothes until somebody let them in on the secret of how to open the bookcase. Some of them must have objected. Kids would have liked it, but . . . Nels couldn't help grinning as he pictured—oh, Tom Curtis's grandfather, or the junior high principal—one of those stiff-starchy grown-ups you couldn't imagine ever being a kid—pictured somebody like that staring indignantly down his nose while one of the butterfly waitresses (or somebody) explained that his clothes closet was behind those books. Or better still, struggling and pounding on the shelves, still in his underwear and late for dinner because he'd forgotten how it opened . . .

Nels gave a laugh and hastily stifled it, though Alice was not likely to hear that if she'd barely heard him yelling a minute ago. And that was odd since noises from the kitchen carried plainly up here. Maybe because sound traveled best upwards? Or maybe the kitchen wasn't directly below. Still, she was down there somewhere—baking cookies, he could smell them—so he must be careful. He must always be careful in this room—leave everything as he'd found it, and above all, close the bookcase when he left. That bookcase was going to be the secret of secrets, the part he could keep absolutely his own. Even if somebody discovered that east wing passage behind the screen, and walked into this room—why, he could leap into that closet and pull the door almost shut . . . being careful not to let it latch, of course. Prudently, Nels tried it first standing where he was, pushing the door until to a casual eye its boxlike frame appeared flat against the wall. Then, with a strange, shivery little thrill, he stepped right inside, and curling his hand around the edge he pulled the bookcase slowly toward him until it caught his fingers. But that left it nowhere near closed; groping, he found a coat hook on the back of the door—for the hotel guest's bathrobe, presumably—which served as a sort of handle to draw it closer. The last crack of light disappeared, and the door came to rest against its latch mechanism, but he could tell it would take a firm tug to make it fasten. Safe as churches. Nels swung it wide again and stepped out, exhilarated.

Below, the oven door was whine-screeching again, and he could hear voices from out on the driveway—Rory's and Stevie's. He'd better not stay longer. There was still tomorrow. And the next day. The whole summer. Yesterday it had stretched before him as an endless desert; now it budded and bloomed. Meanwhile, here were all these books and knick-knacks still scattered over the floor.

He began to put everything back, briefly examining each object before replacing it on a shelf, glancing into each book, without quite knowing what clue he looked for. But several theories were forming in his mind. Theory One—this was surely the General's old room. There were three thick volumes titled *On War*, by somebody named Von Clausewitz, and one about military aircraft, as well as that brass shell casing. As for Theories Two and Three, he'd better pump Alice.

He finished his job—it was warm work; next time he'd open a window—and swung the bookcase door shut, pressing until he heard the muffled *click*. At once he was sure he couldn't open it again. How had he done it? Not by pulling. He'd given a sort of *shove* on the right-hand edge, and then let go. Firmly he shoved and let go again, and heard the *click* as its latch released. Weak with relief, he pushed it closed once more.

A last glance around assured him that the room again seemed undisturbed, though some of the dust was on him now, and the books no doubt were in different positions. Silently he moved down the little east passage, leaving the door with the mirror half-open as he'd found it, and after a cautious peek through the carved screen, slipped around it into the hall. In another minute he had made it to the west wing bathroom and was prosaically washing his hands.

CLEAN AND MUCH COOLER, Nels drifted into the kitchen a few moments later as if drawn only by the cookie fragrance he had already got a whiff of upstairs. Here it was all-powerful—warm, sweet, nutmeg-y, faintly tinged with the charred smell of the inevitable burnt batch.

"Now what could've brought you, I wonder," Alice said without looking around from the center worktable, where she was cutting out another row of circles. "By the way, was it you calling me, a little while ago?"

"Calling you? No," Nels answered with just the right blend

of good manners and indifference—and with perfect truth.

"Somebody was," Alice grumbled. "Was calling *somebody*. Oh, well, if you're going to pester and pester like that, I suppose you can have a couple of those brown ones."

Nels selected the two least overdone cookies and leaned back against the counter where the rest were spread out to cool, taking a large and crunchy mouthful. When he was able to speak again he said carelessly, "Hey, I was wondering. You know that old colonel or general or something you said used to live here?"

"General," Alice said. "Brigadier General P.L. Rutherford, Retired. Yes, what about him?"

"Well, I just wondered which room was his."

"East room. Right above here," Alice answered, neatly confirming Theory One. "Got its own bath just across the east passage."

"That sounds nice."

"Suited him, anyway. He spent his last nine, ten years there, hardly went further than the post office." Alice wadded the scraps of dough into a ball and rolled it flat, adding, "Nice old coot. Kinda peculiar but aren't we all? I liked him, the little time I knew him."

"Little time? Nine or ten years?"

"*He* was here all those years. I didn't say I was."

"Oh," Nels said blankly. He couldn't picture Alice anywhere but the Inn. "Then where were you?"

"Why, I'd left to get married. More fool I. I was real busy being Mrs. Eldon E. Clary of Easterside for quite a spell there." Alice's tone was tarter than usual as she carried the sheet of cookies to the oven. "But I was back before Maureen was out of diapers. The General was only here three years after that." She closed the oven door—it made the whine-screech Nels had heard upstairs—and straightened, smiling. "He used to jump rope. I mean it—seventy-nine years old and he jumped twenty-five turns every morning to keep in shape. I could hear his toes tapping up yonder, when I'd be getting breakfast. Twenty-five taps exactly. And walk! He'd walk up and down that room, up and down."

She raised her eyes to the high, dimly green ceiling, and Nels did too. "Must be an awful big room," he remarked.

"Oh—about the size of this one, I guess. It's right up above."

"Then what's above the pantry and the dining room?" Nels asked quickly.

Alice frowned, squinted around the boundaries of the ceiling again, then gave it up with a shrug. "Darned if I know. Seems like there used to be some other rooms up there, in the old days—a whole suite, wasn't it? Then they remodeled . . . I think they did shut off a section of this wing, so's not to have to heat it. But Lord, that was twenty years ago. I can't remember what all they did. Look, Buster, could I get you to move on somewhere else now? I've got pies to make yet, and I'm not doing much but talk."

Nels willingly moved on, having fairly established Theory Two: the General's room was once part of a suite. He wanted to walk entirely around the Inn on the outside now, and try to spot those shut-off rooms. He was remembering the huge, ornate piece of furniture blocking the end of the east passage. It might well hide a nailed-shut door once leading to smaller rooms right next to the General's—maybe a dressing room and bedroom—which in the old days opened *into* the General's, *through a connecting door now remodeled into a bookcase-closet!* It was all beautifully logical—even explaining why the General's room lacked an ordinary closet: it had probably been the sitting room of the suite.

Letting himself out the back door, he started his tour of inspection along the rear of the Inn, past the Rooftop Realty offices, across the weedy flagstones of the one-time terrace, on behind the store where the old apple trees grew, and clear around the west wing, past the flagged front walk, to the big bay window where the game table stood. Here he halted, staring up at the building and trying to map its interior in his head. To this point he could match everything, identify every window.

Only the east wing was mysterious. It was narrower on top, as if the second storey had shrunk; the strip of flat kitchen roof he'd looked down on from the General's windows stuck out like a shelf all along that side. So the General's room wasn't *directly* above the kitchen as Alice thought, but stair-stepped back. There were two windows facing front—those would be the north ones flanking the General's desk—but then came *three more* windows, roughly above the dining room. What room was that, if not part of the shut-off suite? And what about that turret thing, that squatty little tower with the witch's-hat roof, poking up above everything? Well, maybe the turret was just an ornament like the iron railings. It had a fancy pattern of shingling, and a spidery-thin weathervane on top, shaped like a new moon. But were merely ornamental turrets that large? This one had what looked like little gabled windows all around—or as far around as Nels could see by backing up nearly to the road. They looked like real windows. So were there real rooms up in the tower too? If so, how did you get to them, if not through those blocked-off rooms next to the General's—or from the General's room itself?

Maybe that tower showed better from the service yard. Nels was about to walk around back to find out, when Stevie came running from somewhere on the other side of the road, hailing him gladly.

"Hey, Nels! You all through reading? Hey, look what I found, over there under the railroad trestle in those weeds. Isn't he pretty, though?" Stevie extended a palm, carefully cupped to hold a small and dapper beetle—elegantly gold and black, with stripes on his wing cases and spots on his front.

"Yeah, he is," said Nels, momentarily distracted. Automatically he reached for the tiny captive, but Stevie jerked his hand back.

"No! I don't want a pin stuck through this one."

"I wasn't going to do anything but turn him over!" Nels said indignantly. "I'd never stick a pin through a *live* one."

"Well, I don't want this one dead at all. I want to watch him. What kind is he?"

"I don't know. I don't have my book here."

"Gol! You didn't even bring it?" Stevie's face fell into a mask of disappointment.

"No, or the box or any of our other stuff, either. I thought you said you didn't want to collect any more."

"Well, I don't want any more on pins, in boxes. I don't see any use in it. But I still want to know what they *are*. Their names and all."

"How d'you think anybody ever found out what they are without putting them in boxes to classify them?" It was an old argument, and Nels spoke without heat. "It's the scientific method."

"So is watching what they do. Whoops! Don't go yet, Stripey, stick around." Stevie clapped his other hand over the beetle, and with some difficulty got him into a pants pocket. "He can take a nap. What were you looking at up there on the roof?"

"Nothing, just gawking around," Nels said quickly. As Stevie still squinted toward the General's room he added, "Want to go for a bike ride now?"

And that was the last chance he had to be alone that day. By the time he and Stevie got back from their bike ride, the younger ones had come back too, and so had Nels's restlessness and unanswered questions, and the monsters were beginning to surface again. He went to bed promising himself to plan better tomorrow, to get free early and go straight to the east wing. Something was there for him, he knew it—something more than just a private place. What it was or how he would find it was still unclear, but he felt more and more certain that once he did find it, everything might change.

II

THE BOOKCASE

NELS DID NOT get back to the General's room for more than a week, except for a few snatched moments. For one thing, he awoke next morning to find it raining. And it went on raining, steadily and wetly, for four solid days—which meant that Rory and Jenny and Maureen had to stay indoors instead of disappearing out the back door directly after breakfast. After the first hour of having them underfoot in the kitchen, Alice banished the three of them to the second floor, where they took over the upstairs hall. That left Nels a choice of playing checkers with Stevie and trying not to talk about home, or hanging around the kitchen getting in Alice's way himself.

However, on Saturday morning, the third wet day, they were allowed to use the TV set in Uncle Fred's room at the rear of the west wing. In the middle of a loud cartoon, Nels drifted away unnoticed, and sprinted down the long, dim hall. Scarcely believing his luck, he slipped behind the screen and down the passage, his eyes seeking that mirror ahead in spite of all reason. As he reached it, he stepped again on the creaky board.

And in the mirror, the boy turned from the window—he had been leaning on the sill, peering out into the rain—and his eyes met Nels's. They were dark, lively eyes, full of suppressed laughter, and they were unsurprised—as if he had expected Nels. But he spun away out of range at once and the mirror was empty as ever.

"No *wait*!" Nels gasped, flinging himself into the room, his mind in an uproar and his feet clumsy with excitement. There was no one there. He dashed for the bookcase, fumbled with trembling hands and finally calmed himself enough to give the shove-and-release that opened it.

No one inside, either. Just the dim, discolored walls, the broken yardstick. *But he had seen him*. Surely he had seen him?

Drawing a long breath, Nels turned away, hardly knowing whether he was filled with hope or nearly dying of this fresh disappointment. Be patient, he told himself desperately. Just be patient. Maybe next time.

He crossed the room restlessly, shivering a little. No need to open a window today; it was chilly in here, cold and wet outside. Sitting down at the desk, he began after a moment to explore its drawers, which were still full of the General's odds and ends. He had only a brief half-hour before the Saturday lunch bell rang, and he had to steal hastily down the hall to his own room, so that he could stroll out of it casually when the others emerged from their TV session.

Then it was Sunday—a day of rituals almost non-stop. Breakfast was later and larger—though as far as Nels could see, nobody was hungrier for more food, just crabbier from having to wait. Next came baths, and clothes you were warned not to rumple, and the cramped ride through the rain in the Websters' old black Plymouth to the village church. Church for Aunt Ruth and Uncle Fred and Alice; for the children, Sunday school—an eternity of sitting on stiff little chairs in circles of strangers. The Natives, as Nels crossly called their Sunday school classmates, were not friendly. From the Andersons' first Sunday, the local children had elaborately ignored them, reacting to any remark they made with blank surprise, as if a stone had spoken. Not unnaturally, nobody had made more than one.

Once that bondage was over, there was another dressed-up and idle half-hour before Sunday dinner, which gave you ample time to start wearily wishing you were home, then to start wondering where home would turn out to be by the time you were allowed back there, and who would be living there with you, and where the others would be, and who was going to be making all these decisions, and how you could bear to know the answers. Then at last, the long dinner itself. Even Rory was irritable by the time it was over and they were free for whatever amusements they could devise that wouldn't disturb Uncle Fred's nap.

Nels finally escaped to his own room with a book. A little later, realizing that he was actually still alone, he tossed the book aside and ran on tiptoe to the east wing. But he was scarcely inside the passage before he heard Jenny climbing the main stair, accompanied by the high, stifled wail of her sorest hurt-feelings crying. Sighing, but not at all surprised, he retraced his steps. He searched Jenny out in the big linen closet, where she had gone to ground in a miserable little hot heap on the floor, coaxed her along to her own room, washed her flushed and tearful face and managed to find out that Rory was a horrible mean old boy and she hated him, and she hated Maureen too, and all they wanted to do was play games that left her out, or fool her and then laugh, or borrow her tow truck and never give it back.

"Come on, I'll read something to you, shall I?" Nels said, and put in a weary half-hour with little kids' stuff that even Jenny scarcely seemed to be listening to. "What's the matter?" he said finally. "Don't you want to hear this story?"

"No. I want to go home," Jenny told him despairingly. "Why do we have to stay here so long? I don't *like* it here."

"You'll like it again when you can go outdoors, and over to Maureen's and all."

"No I won't. I want Mommie to come. I wish Daddy was here to take us swimming or maybe to the park like he used to. Aren't they *ever* going to come and get us?"

"Sure, only not—right away," Nels said. He had begun to

breathe hard and feel hot and funny around the forehead, and he wished violently that Jenny would shut up.

"Why not? When are they coming, then? I want to go *now*."

"Well, you can't. And it won't be both Daddy and Mommie anyway, only I don't know which one, and we have to stay here until somebody does come, so there's no use going on about it!" Nels jumped up, unable to stay where he was an instant longer, and Jenny dissolved into tears again because he was cross with her. He fled—literally ran—from her misery and his own, and the questions he couldn't answer, leaving her to cry her own way out of it there on her bed. He taught Stevie chess until suppertime.

But finally Sunday, too, was over.

On Monday the sun came out. Right after breakfast the Gleesome Threesome, good tempers and smiles restored as if they had never been absent, headed for the path under the railroad trestle and Maureen's house. By nine-thirty Stevie had pursued a conversation with Uncle Fred clear into the store, and Alice had vanished into the basement to sort the wash. Nels flew up the back stairs, silent and single-purposed. With a swift glance down the empty length of the upstairs hall, he slid behind the screen into the east passage. This time he felt no doubts, no uncertainties; when he reached the mirror, he saw the boy's reflection as he'd known he would. This time the floor did not creak, and Nels did not hesitate. He stepped straight into the room, and as the boy whirled away toward the bookcase, he cried "Wait!" and leaped forward to block his way.

FOR A MOMENT they stood facing each other, their eyes meeting directly for the first time. The boy's dark ones were triumphant, excited—as if *he's* caught *me*, Nels thought. The notion was so odd he almost retreated a step, then remembering how fast the boy could move, hastily flung out both arms. That made the boy grin outright, with such mischief that Nels instantly dropped his hands and stepped aside. He'd outgrown cat-and-mouse games in the fourth or fifth grade, and it might as well be clear from the beginning.

Good-naturedly, the boy shrugged and lost all appearance of wanting to escape. "Don't worry. I won't run away," he said. "I wanted you to catch me, you know. Sooner or later."

"I—sort of thought you did." Nels relaxed too, and let exhilaration take over. It was all happening, exactly as he'd wished it might. There were so many questions crowding into his mind now that it was hard to choose one. "What's your name?" he asked.

"Alan."

Alan. Why, that's my favorite name, Nels thought, feeling the extra little glow that comes with delightful coincidence. It seemed the best of good omens. "Mine is—"

"I already know yours. Nels."

"Oh. How do you know it?"

Alan shrugged again. "Heard them calling you, around here."

Of course, Nels thought. I should have realized. He met the boy's glance; again it held that hint of mischief, as if Alan knew a great many things about him, more than he meant to tell. "My other name's Anderson," he offered. "What's yours?"

"Reeves. Same as in Reeves Ferry."

"Oh. Naturally," said Nels, then wondered why it should seem so natural. "Where did you come from?" he blurted.

Alan merely jerked his head toward the bookcase.

"Yes, but I mean—why do you hide in there?"

"I don't. I live there. I always have."

"You live here at the Inn? In a *closet*?"

Alan laughed. "That's not a closet. Listen, I'll show you. Shall I? Then you won't have to ask so many questions."

"Okay," Nels agreed uncomfortably. Perhaps he had sounded rude. "I did figure out how to open it," he said as they moved toward the bookcase. "Pure accident. But I couldn't see any way out on the other side."

"It's pretty well camouflaged," Alan said easily. He opened the bookcase, stepped unhesitatingly into the dark space, and stood aside. "It just looks like a crack in the plywood—and that big stain helps, too. But it's a door, see?" As he spoke, he pushed with one hand on the rear wall, revealing a thread of light tracing a door-shaped rectangle. Holding it ajar just that crack, Alan glanced back casually, jerked his head. "Better shut the bookcase behind you. Catch hold of that hook thing and pull—just till it barely touches. *Don't latch it*, you hear? Just pull it to."

Suddenly shaky and dry-mouthed with excitement, Nels stepped into the dark after him, and did as he was told. The General's room narrowed to a slice of wallpaper-and-windows, to a slit of bright daylight—then even the slit vanished, though it danced a moment behind Nels's eyelids in luminous green as he stood breathing quickly, still grasping the chilly metal of the coat hook.

"That's the way," came Alan's offhand voice. "Okay—"

"Why shouldn't I latch it?" Nels whispered. Something in him wanted to hear that muffled *click*, close to his ear this time, in the dust-smelling dark. "It'd be all right now. *You* latch it, don't you?"

"That's different, I live here," Alan said sharply. "It's different for me."

A stubborn *why*? trembled unspoken on Nels's lips and his hand lingered on the coat hook. Then the unreasoning flicker of rebellion sputtered out, and his hand dropped. As if he knew it, Alan said cheerfully, "So come on, let's go."

The crack in the back wall widened swiftly into a rectangle of light, with Alan's dark silhouette moving into it, and then beyond it, into a room. Nels had an impression of color—pale lilac, a blur of red. Eagerly, he followed.

STEVIE WAS IN the store, leaning against the counter with his chin in both hands, staring up at the big wall calendar above Uncle Fred's head. It showed a picture of some cows in a field, with a lot of daisies in the foreground and a lot of high mountains behind. At one side, back beyond the cows, you could see part of a barn with a steep roof, and a house with flower boxes at the windows and fancy, carved wooden balconies that made Stevie think of the cuckoo clock, at home.

"Where's that supposed to be?" he asked.

Uncle Fred, sitting in his special chair behind the cash register, turned in his slow, stiff-necked, difficult way and finally got his eyes on the calendar. He took his time studying it, which was only fair, thought Stevie, after he took so much trouble to twist around there. Then he said, "Switzerland, young man. That's someplace in Switzerland. Mountains back there are probably the Alps."

"Oh, yeah." Stevie knew what the Alps were, from school. "How come that house is so fancy? Is it some special house?"

"No, no, not necessarily, not necessarily. Just the style of the country. Same in Bavaria. My oh me, you should see all those gingerbread houses in Bavaria. Pretty as a picture."

"Gingerbread *houses*? Like Hansel and Gretel?"

"That's just what they look like. Yep, like Hansel and Gretel." Uncle Fred was slowly swiveling back around now.

"You ever been there?" Stevie asked with interest. "Switzerland and Bavaria and all? Where's Bavaria?"

"In Germany. Oh, yes . . . yes . . . I was there once. When I was a young man."

"Gol! What was it like?"

But Uncle Fred's memories had grown vague, or else his attention had strayed to the stack of sales slips beside the cash register. He began thoughtfully to thumb through them as he said, "Oh—like you see there in the picture. Very much like that. Been a long time now."

Stevie tried a few more questions, but got only absent-minded, though amiable, answers. Uncle Fred was nice, and he knew a lot of interesting things, but it was discouragingly hard to get any of them out of him. Lots of grown-ups were like that, Stevie had noticed. They brought something up *themselves*, then when you wanted to know more, they told you it was too long to go into, or you wouldn't understand it anyway, or else they just let the whole subject sort of evaporate and you never heard of it again.

He sighed, and looked around for something else to do. Rory and Jenny had gone to Maureen's, probably for the day; Nels wanted to read until lunchtime. The only TV program Stevie liked was already over. It was boring to play racing cars all by yourself. And on top of everything, today was Monday. Stevie had no use for Mondays, he never had. He had often thought he could wake up one morning having lost his memory and with no idea who or where he was, and *still* know it was Monday just by the way it felt.

"Uncle Fred, do you like Mondays?" he asked.

"Mondays? Well, I can't say I've got anything against Mondays." Uncle Fred's veiny, knobby hands shuffled the pile of sales slips together, knocking the edges even against the counter. Unexpectedly, he added, "I do remember I always used to think of them as yellow."

"Yellow," repeated Stevie, feeling a momentary lift of pleasure. But the sunny vision didn't last. "I always think of them as a sort of washed-out gray," he said.

"Me oh my!" Uncle Fred chuckled and shook his head. "What day do you like, then?"

"Friday. That's a neat day. It looks like Friday in that picture there with the cows and gingerbread houses. They're not *really* gingerbread, are they?"

"No, no, it's just an expression."

"Our Gram used to make gingerbread for us." Stevie's eyes lingered on the calendar picture, as his thoughts drifted back to a much more Friday sort of time. "Every summer, on her birthday—it was in August. We called it Gingerbread Day. She used to have us all over to her house and give us each a gingerbread man she'd made for us. They were real fancy, with gold paper and candy buttons and all that. Gol, she could really make neat ones."

"That's your father's mother you're speaking of?" said Uncle Fred. "Dead now, isn't she? Died a couple of years ago, or so I thought."

"Yeah," Stevie muttered, with a pang of missing Gram.

"But Mommie makes them for us anyhow, every August second. Hers aren't quite as good as Gram's but they're pretty good." She won't make them this summer, though, he thought. We won't even be home this summer to have them.

He felt suddenly hungry—for gingerbread, for crackers, for anything. At that moment the two women Aunt Ruth had been helping came up to the cash register with their brown paper sacks and sales slips. Stevie moved to the back of the store, where Aunt Ruth was refilling the orange bin, and fussing as usual with the little green crepe paper frills edging each display.

"Aunt Ruth? Can I have a cookie or something, or an apple, or a Coke, or—"

"My conscience! So soon after breakfast? You can't be hungry, not if you ate Alice's nice—"

"Or a carrot, even?" said Stevie desperately. "Or a little package of corn chips, or—"

"Corn chips! Nothing could be less nourishing. You can have an orange, I suppose. And Stevie—hand me that box of thumbtacks on the counter yonder. See, by the tape dispenser."

Stevie found the little round cardboard container and brought it to her, removing its lid. "There's only two."

"That's enough." Aunt Ruth plucked them from the box with one hand, the other still holding a length of the crepe paper frill. "Now you can throw the box away for me—in the wastebasket, *not* on the floor. And take your orange outdoors, I won't want juice all over the—"

"Can I have the little box? Please?"

"Oh, yes, yes, I suppose so. Now take the orange outside, dear, and be careful of your shirt . . ."

It was a really neat box, just right for all sorts of things. Stevie gave it a pleased, proprietary inspection inside and out as he left the store by the customers' entrance and walked down the steps into the cool, fresh day. Then he tucked it in his pants pocket and started across the road, beginning to excavate a hole in the top of his orange. He wished those big guys weren't always around the school playground, hogging all the swings and things. He wished beetles didn't mostly come out at night. He wished Parker's meadow weren't out of bounds for him, or that Nels was around right now to go there with him. The place was full of good insects and things, especially around that rock outcrop. But it was across the freeway and a good quarter-mile beyond. Maybe Rory would want to do something with him now, instead of playing all day with Jenny and Maureen. There were those scraps of lumber they'd collected the other afternoon from the weeds around one of the old blackened wooden supports of the railroad trestle. Ends of two-by-twos, even a few larger pieces. You could build a good road, or airstrip or something. Two of you could. The scraps were still there in a pile where he'd left them, he noticed. Wet now, from the rain, but . . .

Stevie went on under the trestle and along the meandering grass and gravel lane that led nowhere but to Maureen's house. Alice's house, he supposed it was, though she was usually at the Inn. Or maybe it was really Maureen's grandmother's house. She was always there somewhere, a real old lady, real deaf, who did nothing but sit in the kitchen in the middle of a lot of cats, and knit—according to Rory. Stevie had never been inside the place.

The little kids were playing on the old gray-painted front porch, dashing up and down the sagging steps in accordance with some ordered procedure only they could understand, shouting back and forth to each other in urgent tones and occasionally stopping to change the script. It looked pretty dull to Stevie, as well as incomprehensible. They paid no attention to him until he threw away his orange skin and came up to the porch, then Maureen and Jenny yelled in unison.

"Hey! No! You're walking all over the bee jelly! And the silken canopies!" Jenny added wildly. "Get off, get *off*!" She was down the steps now, pushing him, Maureen right behind her.

"Well, gol, don't knock me over!" protested Stevie, stumbling back and apparently stepping straight into something even more precious though invisible, for it raised another anguished chorus. "*I* can't see your dumb canopies or anything!" he told them. "I'm not going to stay anyhow, I just came to get Rory."

"What for? Have I got to go home or something?" Rory asked from the porch steps.

"No, I just—d'you want to build roads, with those pieces of wood, or anything?"

"Oh. Huh-uh, not now," Rory told him. "Maybe after lunch or something."

"Clear after *lunch*?"

"Well, I want to go on playing this. It's my turn to be king."

"Oh, gol! King!"

"So? What's wrong with that?" Rory demanded, turning a little red and frowning. "We're having fun."

"And *you* can't *play*, so go *away*," put in Maureen.

Unexpectedly, Jenny retorted, "Yes, he can! You're not our boss. But he mustn't step on things."

"But he'll want to be king all the time," Rory protested.

"Oh, who wants to play your dumb game anyhow," Stevie muttered, turning away and heading back toward the Inn. To his disgust, tears sprang to his eyes, hot and blurry. He walked faster, scuffing through the weeds and scowling, blinking them away, as behind him the game started up again. What's the matter with me? he thought. I'll just build the road by myself, and get to have *all* the big pieces.

He did build a road of sorts, there under the railroad trestle near the place where they had found the wood. But it wasn't much fun, with nobody to talk to about what this thing was and what that thing was going to be, nobody to add other ideas. Rory always had all these real wild ideas, and the two of them always got to laughing real hard, and that's what made it fun. Oh, *well,* Stevie thought, abandoning the whole project and tossing away his biggest piece of wood. It nearly hit a beetle—a narrow-backed, dull blackish-brownish creature half-hidden under the mold near the old post. Swiftly Stevie was beside it, flipping it onto its back, waiting and watching. It waited too, for a minute, lying quietly as if it meant to stay there forever. Then its forelegs wiggled, and suddenly it gave a loud click, shot seven or eight inches straight into the air and came down right side up, running.

Before it could get far, Stevie flipped it over again, keeping an eye on it while he tugged his thumbtack box out of his pocket, found a bent paperclip in another pocket and punched two or three holes in the lid—surely click beetles needed air?—and captured his specimen in the middle of another flip. Flushed with triumph, he began looking for other kinds of beetles, wondering about a bigger box—a sort of cage box, with little screened-off divisions, where a person could keep things *live*. Maybe he could even find another praying mantis. Once—last fall, it was—he and Nels had kept a mantis as a pet till almost Thinksgiving. They'd caught it in their net—they'd made a *good* net last summer, but he didn't know what had happened to it—and taken it home in a jar, and then just let it go free in their room. All you did to feed it was just hand it a fly or moth or something. It reached right out and sort of took the fly in one hand, and ate it just like you'd eat an ice cream cone. Or not quite—it used to bite off the wings and head first, then eat the rest. And afterwards it washed its face like a cat. Mantises were *great*. They hunted flies on their own, too, which was why Mommie had let him and Nels keep theirs loose in their room. Mommie never objected to spiders, either. She was *for* anything that was *against* flies.

Stevie grinned to himself as he dawdled along, watching the grass for more beetles, then suddenly he wasn't grinning any longer but instead was missing his mother so bad and hard it was like a sharp pain inside him—a knife cutting him, or something being stretched and stretched a lot too far. He felt as if he *had* to hear her say something—just any usual little thing, like "For pity's *sake*" or "Dear old Nels" or "Henny-Jenny"—and if he couldn't, he'd just . . . It seemed a year already since Fourth of July when she came down, and she wasn't coming any more, and he did see why, only . . .

He started in a hurry back to the Inn. He'd find Nels. Maybe go to Parker's meadow to the rock outcrop. Show him the click beetle, anyway—even without the insect book, Nels might remember what sort it was, just by looking at it. Nels knew practically *everything*; he'd read that whole insect book straight through, besides a whole bunch of others about stars and spaceships and robots and stuff. He could draw spaceships—diagrams, sort of—that he invented himself, with all the parts labeled and all, that Dad said were *sophisticated*, which meant really pretty good. Stevie could draw them too, but he didn't exactly understand what he was drawing. All those cones and fans and antennae. The only kind of antennae he really knew much about were the kind that grew on real live insects, and they weren't just boring little boxes, or soup-plate things, but beautiful, thin, thin feathers, or magic wands, or scallopy horns, or like those rolled-up paper things at the fair that you blow into and they shoot out straight, with just a little curl at the end. There were about a million different shapes of antennae—he'd seen a lot of them right in that book. Maybe they could get Mommie to send them the book! Now that was an idea. Nels could write her a letter and ask. Nels wrote real long things all the time, it wasn't a bit hard for him to write letters. Once he even wrote a sort of story.

And when we've got the book here, thought Stevie, bounding up the Inn's steps and attacking the big front door latch in a sort of frenzy, the way you had to, to make it open, then we could make that cage box with screens, and catch a lot of different kinds of things and keep them alive, and still look them up in the book to be scientific.

The door gave at last, and he burst through, already calling Nels, slammed it behind him and called again, louder. Aunt Ruth came to the store door that opened into the main hall and shushed him in a low indignant tone, adding, "My conscience, Stevie! Do try to remember that these are *business* premises, at least during the day!"

"I'm sorry. D'you know where Nels is?" Stevie asked.

"I haven't set eyes on him. Nor *heard* him either," added Aunt Ruth pointedly, and retreated into the store.

Stevie said "Gol!" to himself, and rolled his eyes, then climbed the main stairs two at a time and searched the whole second floor, calling more cautiously, but peeking in all the likely rooms, too, and some unlikely ones. Nels wasn't in any of them. He wasn't even way back behind that carved thing, in the east wing where nobody ever went, though Stevie drifted clear back there, feeling out-of-place and strange because he'd never ventured behind the carved thing before, but figuring Nels—who was so much braver—might. But there was nothing there anyhow, just a spooky little passage and a couple more rooms full of leftover damp chilly air from yesterday. Stevie was glad to go on down the back stairs. He lurked a moment in the passage outside the kitchen, but Alice was alone, banging pans around and singing something to herself which had an angry-sounding refrain that sounded like, "And *I* don't care, if you was me . . . Hang you high on a boxwood tree!" It couldn't be that, Stevie thought. Anyhow Nels wasn't in there.

Nels wasn't anywhere. Not anywhere a person could find him. As if he was . . . doing it on purpose. Avoiding Stevie.

Stevie stood around in the main hall awhile, feeling the burden of time and time and more time like a trillion pound weight pressing on his shoulders and dragging at his hands and feet. He felt no interest in his click beetle now, or his plans for the box with little cages. The morning had been going on for hours and hours; and no telling how many more would crawl by before lunch. Even lunch would be fascinating by comparison with this—this sudden nothing, this total, absolute absence of anything to do. He glanced toward the long, barren mail table at the foot of the main stairs, but he knew the mail never came till afternoon. Anyhow there almost never was anything—once a week the note from their mother, usually to all four of them together, mostly explaining why she didn't have time to write them oftener, with her job and—all that other stuff, whatever it was. Counseling, and—lawyers. Their father never wrote letters. He sent postcards from airports around the state, wherever he had to fly freight, with pictures of beaches or bear cubs or a salmon or something, and once a box of salt water taffy, and once he had phoned, but it was a real flop. None of them had known what to say. Even Dad hadn't known what to say—he hadn't sounded like himself but like just any other grown-up, a teacher or somebody trying to be nice.

Stevie went over to the game table, thought fleetingly of trying to play checkers by himself, then stared a long time out the little panes of the bay window. Finally he dawdled back down the passage and out the back door, climbed on his bicycle, feeling like some kind of boring wind-up toy, and pedaled slowly down the driveway to the road.

4.

"THE FACT IS, it always was our house," Alan said, fitting a triangular piece of stripey blue neatly into the sky of the jigsaw picture. "At least this part with the tower was ours. The whole east wing, upstairs and down. They just built the rest of the Inn onto it when they wanted to make the hotel."

"Well, it's great!" Nels glanced around Alan's room, which was shaped like a piece of pie with the point cut off, the door in the cut part and windows along the outside curve. Clearly, a segment of the tower—so clearly that the logic of it gave a special pleasure, like a math problem working just right.

A strange, sweet bubble of peace rose through Nels, lightening and expanding him until he felt like some sort of jolly balloonman, barely tethered to his chair. Since his very first sight of this tower—just before Stevie had come along the other day and he'd had to quit staring—he'd somehow known he'd find his way to it, and that it was secret, exciting, something just for him.

So far, he scarcely knew anything besides that. They'd rushed up here so hurriedly, he and Alan, that he'd barely glimpsed anything on the way to this room. He was still trying to orient himself, to make what he'd seen from outside fit what he saw in here.

He said, "I thought Uncle Fred said his father built the whole Inn building. Or his grandfather or somebody. I thought that meant this east part too."

"He probably said 'remodeled.' They remodeled our part,

then just built the rest on. Hey, is that piece under your elbow a hunk of chimney? It is!" Alan reached for it, fitted it into his side of the puzzle, and added, "You'd better come to, I'm going to beat you by a mile."

"Yeah, you are," Nels muttered, hastily turning his attention back to the scattered fragments in front of him.

"You're quite a daydreamer, aren't you?" Alan remarked.

Nels glanced at him quickly. But of course Alan couldn't know he was touchy about such comments. "I guess so," he said in a careless tone. "My mom calls it 'woolgathering.' I can't help it. I take after my dad." But when Mom said that, it was almost an accusation, as if he *could* help it if he'd only try. *Impractical dreamers, the pair of you!* He could hear the despair in her voice. *Really, Nels, why can't you be trusted to remember to*—to start the potatoes, or go after milk, or some other chore he was supposed to do before she got home.

"What's woolgathering?" Alan jiggled a bit of rooftop into place.

Nels moved restlessly, wishing Alan would drop the subject. "Oh—just thinking about something else, I guess. Instead of what she wants me to be thinking about. I can't see anything wrong with it—why shouldn't I think about what *I* want to sometimes, instead of always having to—"

"I don't see anything wrong with it either," Alan broke in disarmingly. He grinned at Nels, who presently grinned back, feeling his discomfort ease and the soothing sensation of weightlessness steal over him again. "So what *were* you thinking about?" Alan went on. "Instead of the puzzle?"

"Well—this tower. Naturally." As Alan glanced at him with innocently raised eyebrows, Nels added, "Come on! You've got to admit the whole thing is sort of . . . weird. How we got here, and you living here, and—well, everything."

"Is it? It seems just ordinary to me."

"Ordinary? To go in and out of your house through a bookcase instead of a door?"

Alan gave in and laughed. "Well, I'm used to it. I can see it might seem funny to you. What do you want to know about it? I'll tell you."

"Okay, then how *did* we get here? Exactly?"

"Why, don't you remember? Into the bookcase-closet, then out through that door in its back wall, up the stair—"

"But—wait a minute. The stair."

"*You* know. An iron stair. Spiral. Real narrow. Ends up right in the hall out yonder." Alan jerked his head toward the door.

"Yes, but where does it start? That's what I can't quite . . . I mean, it doesn't start right from the back of the bookcase, does it?"

"Oh, no . . . there's a sort of room . . . you remember."

It was precisely what Nels couldn't remember. A blurred impression of color, that was all he had of that "sort of room." "Is it at the front, over the dining room?" he persisted. "Is it one of those rooms they closed off when they remodeled?"

But Alan's attention had returned to the puzzle, which he was suddenly finishing in a series of brilliant pounces. "There! I knew if I could find that piece with the cows in it, the rest would go together like nothing. Only one piece of sky missing—sort of wedge-shaped."

"Here it is," Nels said, discovering it in his hand. He dropped it into place and stared in some surprise at the finished result. He had not noticed before what picture was forming—in fact, he had paid very little heed to the clutter of jigsaw pieces, his thoughts having been fully occupied with his own real-life puzzle. Now his attention was riveted.

"Well? That clear it up for you?" asked Alan in triumph.

"Why, it's the Inn!" Nels exclaimed. "Or anyway part of it . . . your family's part?"

"Our original house."

"Sure, I see now. Only it's got a pasture behind it. And fruit trees all around."

"That's how it was, to begin with—there's still a few apple trees out back, you know."

"You mean it was a farm once?"

"I guess so—they had cows." Alan had turned vague again, or perhaps lost interest. Abruptly he brought both hands swooping down upon the puzzle, lifted it high, and let it fall back upon the table in a jumble, as Nels exclaimed in protest.

"Hey, wait! Why did you do that?"

"Oh, I was tired of it. Anyway, it was all finished, wasn't it?"

"Yes, but . . . I wanted to look at it some more."

"Oh, well." Alan shrugged rather impatiently, and began scooping the pieces by handfuls into the old shoebox it had come out of. "We can put it together again tomorrow, if you want to. Let's play something else for a change. After I get us some lemonade. Are you thirsty?"

Nels discovered that he was extremely thirsty. "Lemonade would taste great. Shall I come help you?" he added, on his feet with alacrity as Alan headed for the door.

"Oh, no, I'll bring it," Alan said carelessly. "Won't take a minute." But his parting smile at Nels, as the door closed behind him, was more mischievous than polite.

He knew I wanted to come, Nels thought, chagrined. He doesn't mean for me to see the rest of the tower yet. Well, I want to! What's to stop me just opening that door and . . . But maybe he's teasing.

Remembering that parting grin, Nels felt this much more likely. Alan was probably standing on the other side of the door this minute, waiting for him to tiptoe closer, watching for the knob to turn carefully, quietly . . . and the door would be locked. Or it would open, and there would be Alan right outside, laughing his head off.

Nels turned his back firmly on the door, half-piqued, half grudgingly amused. He could remember playing such tricks on Stevie sometimes, when they were both younger. Never mind. Here was a good chance to examine this room more closely. It seemed an ordinary enough room: faded wallpaper, built-in bunk beds, a wall cupboard, and over between the windows the big scarred table where they'd done the puzzle. The windows were casement style, and one was open. Nels walked to it quickly, looked straight down onto a steep, sloping roof, then down again—his stomach knotted from the roller-coaster effect—to a shelf of flat roof sticking out below that, trimmed with pointy iron railing. That would be the kitchen roof. Below that, he could see just a strip of the graveled driveway. Clear enough. It all fitted with the house he'd seen in the puzzle. How could this tower have seemed so small to him, that day he'd first looked up at it from outside? In the puzzle picture it was big—a dominant feature of the house. And it was obviously set just above the rooms once connecting with the General's room, whose existence he had deduced the day he first opened the bookcase.

From his high perch, Nels suddenly saw Stevie appear from beneath the corner of the kitchen roof and pedal disconsolately down the drive. He recoiled as if the window had burned him; simultaneously the door opened behind him and Alan said, "I hope you like it kind of sour. There wasn't much sugar. D'you mind drinking it out of teacups?"

"Oh. Sure. That's okay." Still Nels lingered near the window, watching as the bicycle meandered its lonely way toward the road, annoyed at himself for feeling guilty. "There goes Stevie," he couldn't help saying.

"Where?" Alan set the two cups down on the table and stepped to the opened window, hanging half out of it to crane toward the road. Before Nels could stop him he was waving both arms and yelling, "Whooop! Hey, Stevieeeeee!"

"Stop!" Nels gasped. "Get back! Shut *up*." He seized Alan's arm and tried to pull him away.

Alan only laughed and resisted, even grabbing Nels in return and tugging him toward the window, shouting, "Here we are! Hey, Stevie! Up here, up here!"

"Be *quiet*!" Nels was half-frantic, trying to free himself and restrain Alan at the same time. "Alan, please! What are you doing? You'll spoil everything!"

"No, I won't." Suddenly ceasing to struggle, Alan allowed himself to be hauled back into the room. He faced Nels, still flushed with laughter. "Relax," he drawled. His expression was impish. "I was only teasing you. He can't even hear me."

"How do you know he can't? And anyhow, what if he looked *up*?"

"He wouldn't see a thing."

"But—!" Nels, torn between indignation and bewilderment, broke off to stare at Alan. "What do you mean, he wouldn't see a thing?"

"Just—he wouldn't notice anything." Alan shrugged and turned quickly away. "You can't see these windows very well from down there. Come on, let's drink this lemonade before the ice melts."

Without answering, Nels followed him to the couch. It was true Stevie might not notice anything. Stevie tended to observe microscopically at ground level, and miss almost everything above. Anyway, he was busy riding his bike right now. And he probably wouldn't want to come up here, it wasn't the sort of thing he—

"Quit worrying," Alan said, handing him a rose-patterned

teacup. "It's against the rules around here." He met Nels's eyes and added with peculiar firmness, "Nobody will see me. Take my word." Then he took a big gulp of lemonade and made a face. "A little sour. But not bad, considering I made it myself. What would you like to do?"

"How come, you made it yourself?" Nels asked. "Do you—do you live here alone?"

"Alone? Of course not!" Alan gave a laugh and stared at him.

"Well—I got to wondering. Who does make it usually, then?"

"My mother. But she's not around this morning. Probably gone to get sugar," Alan added with a grin.

"Who else lives here, besides you and her?"

"Just my dad. I'm the only child, if that's what you're getting at. No brothers, sisters, cats, dogs, or other bad habits. Peaceful, that's what it is. Just my parents and me."

Parents, plural, Nels thought, wondering if the odd tremor that swept him was envy, or an obscure, profound relief. Naturally Alan wouldn't live here alone! What a dumb thing to wonder—just because his mother wasn't in sight right now. How often was Tom Curtis's mother in sight? Practically never.

In fact, it might be dumb to keep asking questions. Just wait, and let things gradually come clear—that was better. Insisting on explanations too hard, too soon, might really spoil things—every instinct told him so. And that would be unthinkable.

He asked no more questions that morning. They played chess when they'd finished the lemonade—it was exhilarating, to find an opponent who was neither much better than you, like Dad, nor too impatient, like Tom Curtis, nor a complete beginner you had to teach instead of play with, like Stevie. Alan was an even match for him, Nels found, and the game took on a battle-of-wits element it had lacked before. He won, but just barely. Standing up to stretch, he glimpsed a flash out the window from something down in the road. It turned out to be sunlight glancing off Stevie's handlebars as he came dawdling his snakelike course back toward the Inn. Guiltily Nels glanced at his watch. Eleven-twenty.

"I've got to go," he said. "Right now! I didn't realize—I probably stayed too long."

"Not for me," Alan assured him. "Can you come back tomorrow?"

"Sure! If it's not—inconvenient?"

Alan laughed outright at him. "I'm always here. And look—we've got to pick things up before you go. Every single time." He reached for the empty teacups and started out of the room. "Sorry, but it's a rule around here, and my mom's really set on it."

"Oh, I don't mind," Nels said quickly. He scooped the chessmen into their box, gathered up game board and puzzle box. When Alan reappeared he was shutting the cupboard door. "We didn't scatter much around today."

"Didn't have time," Alan said with a grin. "Come on, I'll take you down now. Get here a little earlier tomorrow, okay?"

"I'll try." Nels smiled back and followed him, longing for it to be tomorrow already.

As rapidly as they had come, they ran down the spiral stair and across the room below. There was no chance at all to look around. Never mind, it's just as well, Nels thought as they plunged into the darkness of the closet behind the bookcase. I'm in a hurry—besides, I'm coming back tomorrow. But he stood eyeing the thin crack of light that edged the bookcase door, hating to widen it. Out there was the ordinary daylight, the ordinary world. And now he could scarcely believe in the tower up above here, Alan's room, the lemonade—any of it.

"Did I just daydream it all?" he said so softly that Alan,

beside him, whispered, "What?" At least Alan himself was really there—or seemed to be. Nels turned to peer at him through the dark, and came out with it, bluntly. "Are you real? Or did I just invent you? Tell the truth."

Alan gave the ghost of a laugh, but answered without hesitation. "I'm as real as you," he said distinctly. "So quit worrying. See you tomorrow—so long!"

"So long!" Reassured, Nels pushed open the bookcase door. There would be plenty of time to play checkers with Stevie before lunch.

III

THE TOWER

IT WASN'T all that easy to "come up earlier" as he'd promised Alan. Nels tried, but the next few mornings he felt lucky when he could get away at all after breakfast. There were always chores like making your bed or collecting your laundry for Alice (usually Jenny's and Rory's too,) or finding something for Stevie in Uncle Fred's encyclopedia ("—Why can't *you* look up Bavaria?" Nels had said in exasperation. But he was doing it for him as he spoke.) And most mornings, there were delays you couldn't foresee or prevent, such as having to get a splinter out of Jenny's knee for her.

"It's *not* that bad, Jenny," he said patiently on Tuesday, as he always had to when the need for this particular minor surgery arose. She would never let anybody but Nels so much as touch the wound—not her mother, not the school nurse, certainly not Alice. It had to be Nels.

"Okay, so let's go find the needle," Nels said when her tears had subsided to gulps. "I don't know where you get so many splinters anyhow," he added as they started for the bathroom. "You ought to learn to get them out yourself, Jenny."

"I'd ruther you did it," she told him—as she always did.

"But sometime I might not be here!" Nels broke off, then finished in a mumble. "I might not always—be around."

"I'd just wait till you got home," Jenny said comfortably.

Nels sighed. She had done exactly that on several occasions. But what about next year, Nels thought helplessly. What if Dad and I . . . "Okay! Sit on the edge of the tub, there," he ordered in a sharper voice than he'd intended, and got busy rummaging in the medicine cabinet for the alcohol. But by the time he'd got the splinter out and soothed Jenny's fresh tears and put on a big Band-Aid for her to be proud of, it was nearly ten o'clock. He found himself alone then, and ran quickly to the east wing, and Alan was waiting in spite of everything. But they had only enough time for a game of chess and another go at the jigsaw puzzle before Nels had to leave.

The next morning, he didn't get there at all, because Alice took Maureen to the dentist in Easterside, leaving Nels in charge of the others until midafternoon. She had also left them a picnic lunch, but the day was overcast, and Aunt Ruth said it was too chilly to eat outside, so they ended up with a boring picnic in the kitchen.

"Oh, well," Stevie said. "It's Wednesday. We'll have a letter from Mommie when the mail comes. Hey, Nels, did you ever write her to send that book?"

"I forgot—I'll wait till tonight. Then I can answer whatever she said today."

But the weekly letter failed to arrive that Wednesday, and the disappointment made all of them cross. Nels had a dozen arguments to settle in the course of the afternoon, of the sort that really required King Solomon, and the rest of the day seemed endless.

Thursday he got away.

And it was just as great as the first time, maybe better, to feel the weightless, carefree sensation take over, and look out over the landscape from Alan's window as if he were high up in a plane or a spaceship or something, and knew he didn't have to think about anything hard or worrisome for a while. He'd got away fairly early, too. By the time they were drinking their lemonade from the rose-patterned teacups, they'd already won a chess game apiece and were ready for something new.

"What sort of things do you like to do?" Alan asked, wiggling his cup to make the ice tinkle. "And don't just say 'anything,' name some."

Nels, who had been about to say, "Oh, anything," smiled and nudged his brain into action. "Well, I play checkers and ride bikes with Stevie, and play Old Maid and stuff like that with Rory and Jenny, and last summer Stevie and I collected insects—"

"I didn't ask what *they* like to do. What do *you* like to do? Don't you ever do anything without them?"

"Sure!" Nels was suddenly on the defensive, without knowing quite why. "I read, and sometimes I draw things—certain kinds of things—and my friend and I across the street do stuff together, like go swimming, or print newspapers with his printing press—"

"I've got a printing press," Alan put in.

"You have?"

"Sure. You mean one of those little hand presses? I've got a pretty good one."

"Oh, *boy*. I mean, Tom and I'd barely got started when I had to leave, and—"

"We'll haul mine out later if you want to. What do you like to read—what kinds of things?"

"Mostly stuff about science—especially electronics. And astronomy. And space exploration, and rockets and all. And science fiction."

"Yeah, me too. What are the 'certain kinds of things' you like to draw?"

"Oh, just—diagrams, sort of. You know, spaceships and all. And inventions I dream up. I don't suppose they'd really work," Nels added deprecatingly.

But Alan seemed fascinated. "Inventions of your own? What kind?"

"Well, different types of robots—you know, real robots, not

the comic strip kind, but machines that can do jobs. For instance, I was working on one that would be programmed to clean house and do the laundry." Nels grinned at Alan's peal of laughter. "Well, I asked my mom for an idea, and that's what she said she wanted."

"What about airplanes? D'you ever draw those?"

Nels glanced at Alan, startled again by the bull's-eye accuracy of his apparently random shots. He drained his cup and reached to put it on the table. "I used to. I drew them all the time—last year. Why?" he asked warily.

"No reason. Just had a hunch you might be an airplane nut." Alan's voice was bland. "D'you like to build things?"

He couldn't mean things like Stevie's and Rory's bridges. All Nels could think of besides was the boring Shop course at school. "You mean like—birdhouses, and footstools?"

Alan nearly choked on the last of his lemonade. "No! I mean like airplanes!"

"Do I like to build airplanes?" Nels said, staring. "I never built any. Oh, you mean models!"

"No, I don't mean models." Setting his cup aside, Alan stood up. "I'm building one now. D'you want to see it?"

"Sure. Where is it?"

Alan grinned. "Look above you."

Nels obeyed, and stumbled to his feet, exclaiming. Directly above his head, hovering—it appeared—just under the high ceiling, was a bright red airplane of a sort he had never see outside a comic strip—or a book about World War II. To be accurate, he had never seen one like *this* anywhere. It was nearly as long as the couch, shaped like a fat cigar with four little propeller blades encircling its nose and two stubby wings sweeping up from under its belly. The cockpit was open, though a sort of sketchy cage constructed of heavy wire replaced the plexiglass bubble. Painted on the underside of each wing was a wide flat ring, like a lifesaver, in deep blue edged with white.

"It's a British Spitfire—more or less," Alan said, heading briskly for the wall cupboard. "What do you think of it?"

"It's just—*great*," said Nels, who was nearly speechless. "How did you ever, *ever*—"

"Oh, I had some help. Dad got me started. And he rigged the landing gear. I'd never have thought of that."

Alan was fiddling with two sets of thin ropes—or thick cords—dangling down alongside the cupboard, so nearly concealed in its shadow that Nels had never noticed them. They ran straight up the wall, he saw, past the top of the cupboard frame to the high ceiling, then straight across the ceiling to the plane, where they were probably attached somehow. Nels had opened his mouth to ask how, when Alan said, "Here she comes!" and the plane slid downward, jerkily at first, then under smooth control, suspended from its tackle like a spider descending on its thread.

"Pulleys!" Nels exclaimed, squinting toward the ceiling, then at the plane, now hovering just above the floor. "Neat!"

"Old Venetian blind hardware, and fishline," Alan said. He was smiling with a satisfaction Nels found easy to understand. "Want to give me a hand? Just bring the nose-wheel assembly from that cupboard—bottom shelf—and set it underneath. . . That's it. Little more to the left, maybe. Now, watch your head."

Nels stepped back to avoid the wing, and Alan lowered the plane the last couple of feet until the fusilage settled on the nose-wheel assembly, and the tiny tail wheel—it looked as if it might have started life on a roller skate—rested on the floor.

"It's great! It's just *great*!" Nels repeated, trying to examine everything about the plane at once.

"Yeah, I like it too. Here, did you notice the instrument

panel?" Alan scrambled onto the wing, then between the cage ribs and into the cockpit with the ease of habit. "Climb in, you can see it better."

"You can *sit* in it! Boy, I never imagined . . . Will it hold us both?"

"Sure, it's strong! Did you think it was just to look at?"

"Well, I didn't know." Nels hoisted himself to the other wing, slid with care into the cockpit beside Alan. The seats were only old cushions, but the instrument panel was a marvel of ingenuity, set with rows of knobs and dials—pressure and electrical gauges, temperature and air-speed indicators, tachometer, altimeter, machmeter, even an artificial horizon. Only at second or even third glance did this impressive array resolve itself into an assortment of empty spools, buttons, Mason jar lids, medicine bottle caps, the cutout tops of coffee cans, scraps of wire and foil and bits of what looked like several defunct clocks—every item so convincingly disguised with paint that it took Nels quite a while to identify them all.

For a time they were both too absorbed in the plane—in discussing it, experimenting with it, getting in and out of it and hoisting it up and down, to think of anything else at all. But eventually even Nels ran out of questions and stood admiringly silent, merely staring at it.

Beside him, Alan sighed. "The only trouble is, it's almost finished. I've only got to paint the cockpit hood . . . and if I could just find something that would make it look like a real plexiglass bubble—"

"What about plastic wrap—that stuff that comes in rolls?" Nels suggested. "Would your mother have some in the kitchen?"

"I don't think so." Alan's manner had gone vague, as it had an odd, sudden way of doing now and then.

Nels thought a minute. A painter's drop sheet? No—too heavy."

"I've got it! Plastic bags. Those big ones you get at the cleaner's."

"But they're dangerous," Nels objected. "We're not supposed to play with them. Kids have got smothered to death."

"Ah, phooey," Alan scoffed. "That's only little kids. We know enough not to put them over our heads, don't we?"

"That's just where they'll *be*, over our heads," Nels pointed out, though without much conviction. After all, the framework of the "bubble" would support the plastic. "I suppose it would be safe enough, really. Have you got some of them around?"

"No. You'll have to bring a couple tomorrow. You *can* come tomorrow, can't you?"

"Well—I hope so. I'll try *hard*," Nels added, his gaze lingering on the plane. "Only I don't know whether I can find any cleaner's bags by then. I don't know where Aunt Ruth keeps anything."

"Alice'll tell you," Alan said confidently. He walked to the cords dangling beside the cupboard and hoisted the airplane partway up. "I want to fix that tail wheel better. You want to help me?"

"I'd better go," Nels said guiltily. "Stevie'll be coming back from his bike ride. I probably ought to be downstairs when he gets here."

"Why?" Alan, securing the cords, turned a puzzled stare over his shoulder.

"Oh, he'll expect it. I'm usually around."

"So what if you are? All the more reason to take a vacation sometimes." Alan gave a little laugh. "No law about it, is there? Don't go yet! Stay till time for lunch, why not?"

Why not? Nels asked himself, and could find no reasonable

answer, only a lift of fresh anticipation and a feeling of reprieve. He thought, it's probably near noon anyhow, then said, "You talked me into it," and went eagerly to help Alan work on the wheel.

For some reason, it was twice as much fun after that. Alan's obvious pleasure in Nels's company was flattering as well as satisfying because Nels felt exactly the same pleasure in his. It was as if the plane had opened a dozen new lines of communication between them, and bypassed whole stages of the getting acquainted process. I don't talk this easily even to Tom Curtis, Nels told himself in astonishment. By the time the lunch bell sounded, distant but clear enough, he felt he knew Alan twice as well as he had just an hour or so before.

"You'll come tomorrow?" Alan said, as he hoisted the plane to the ceiling again and hastily fastened the cords.

"Right after breakfast," Nels promised. He was carrying the nose-wheel assembly to the cupboard, and Alan snatched up the empty teacups and dashed out with them, suddenly in a hurry.

"That's good enough," he said when he reappeared. "Only the chess stuff left—" He swept that into the drawer of the worktable and slammed it shut. "Come on." Then he was hustling Nels out and across the little hall and down the spiral stair and across that room below and into the dark of the bookcase-closet almost before he could collect his wits.

"What's the big rush?" Nels protested, bewildered, as they came to a halt in the stuffy dark.

"Shhh. Sorry—just didn't want to make you late." Alan's lowered voice sounded as if he were smiling. "We don't want anybody nosing around here hunting for you."

"No," agreed Nels quickly. "No, we don't! So long, then—see you tomorrow." His hand touched the bookcase door, and Alan was gone.

BEFORE THE END of another week, Nels had discovered that the quarter-hour after breakfast was the time to vanish. If he left it much later, he found it difficult to get away at all. As it was, he fought a daily battle with his own feeling of guilt toward Stevie, toward all of them, for even wanting to get away. Why shouldn't I do something on my own for once? he argued inwardly. I'm not their parent! . . . *You're the oldest, Nels.* But they do what *they* like! I'm not stopping them! . . . But all Stevie seemed to want to do lately was be with him—just *be* there, depending, expecting. As if he thought I could do something about—everything, Nels thought with the familiar dragging, burdened feeling. I'm tired of being the oldest! he told himself wildly. I can't do it any more! I'm a kid too!

That didn't change a thing. Deep down he couldn't help admitting that if he'd had an older brother, he'd have been clinging too. On Wednesday, when he hurried down to lunch after an exhilarating morning with Alan, and saw the relief and welcome on Stevie's face, the weight of guilt that dropped down on him seemed too great a price to pay even for the tower. I won't go up there tomorrow, he resolved. I'll spend the whole day with Stevie, every bit.

But after lunch the mail came. Their father had sent four packets of candy—chocolate for Jenny, licorice and peppermint for Rory and Stevie, and for him a box of those special tiny French fruit drops only Dad ever remembered he liked—and a card saying, "All I ever see around this place is grown-ups. I sure do miss you guys." There was also a letter apiece from their mother. Nels's said, "Please, Nels, write now and then to keep me posted on how you all are . . . I'll be so glad when I can have you back!" Plenty of mail, for once. But instead of feeling happier he somehow wound up feeling pulled this way and that like a rag doll. He wondered how he could wait till morning, to get away from everything and everybody, and back to the tower.

It was that next morning that he learned how to vanish good and early. From then on, he followed the same routine. The secret lay in making his bed *before* breakfast, and at the same time casually doing whatever other chores he could—and just letting the others go. After breakfast, he had merely to leave the dining room with everybody else, climb the main stairs and amble along to his room wearing the woolgathering expression they were all accustomed to. By then Uncle Fred and Aunt Ruth were usually busy opening the store, Rory and Jenny were heading outdoors with Maureen, and Stevie was starting for the bathroom. Some days the timing was close; if Rory dawdled or Stevie was brisk, there might be only a moment between the time one clattered down the stairs at last, and the other emerged from the bathroom door.

But a moment was all Nels needed to sprint silently down the hall, slide behind that magic wooden screen and hurry on to the General's room, where Alan was always waiting with the bookcase-door ajar. Often they stayed awhile in the General's room, getting acquainted with his books or making use of his desk, careful to keep their voices to a whisper and their movements soundless. But sooner or later a downstairs voice would call, "Anybody seen Nels?" or they'd hear footsteps out in the hall, or their own stealth would begin to seem hilarious, and they'd make for the bookcase, Alan reminding him—as if he needed it—about the latch. Another instant and they were safe away, smothering their laughter as they dashed across the room behind the bookcase—Nels never got a good look at that room—and up the spiral stair to the six-sided hall. Then everything was all right—secure, delightful, busy.

The plane was finished; they had worked together on it several mornings, painting the bubble framework scarlet to match the rest, then stretching over it the plastic cleaner's bag Nels had come across by sheer good luck in the downstairs coat closet. One bag turned out to be enough. They were careful handling it, and no harm came of it. The effect was marvelous—so real even they were astonished at first. Nels had remarked that the plane reminded him of a dragonfly—a scarlet kind called *Sympetrum rubicunculum* he'd seen last summer in a book—and Alan liked that so well they named the plane "Ruby" and painted a dragonfly on the underside of the wing instead of the Spitfire emblem. Then they gave the plane a rest and got out Alan's printing press, and Nels could scarcely decide which was more fun. So far, they had published a one-sheet newspaper, and were now on their third page of a projected science magazine called—after exhaustive discussion—simply *A.M.*, since they were together to work on it only between breakfasttime and lunch.

"Only I still think it ought to say something about science. Or at least about this tower," Nels remarked one morning as he studied the title page they'd proofed the day before.

"Oh, well, we can always change it if we think of something. Look at this—we've got the d's and b's mixed up again."

"Uh-oh." Nels leaned over the worktable, set between the windows for light, where Alan was checking through the flat typecase, picking up minute pieces of rubber type in his tweezers, peering at them, and either putting them back where he got them or changing them to a different section of the many-compartmented tray. "Want me to help you sort them?" he offered nobly.

"No, it won't take me long. You go ahead and set the headlines for my nova article."

Nels agreed with relief, then added, "What nova article?"

"The one I'm going to write as soon as I finish here," Alan said with a laugh. "Just title it something like 'Nova Stars,' and whatever subtitle you can think of, and my name under that, okay?"

"Okay." Nels turned with pleasure to the other typecase. He'd never had proper headline type to use before—in fact, he'd never had nearly this amount or variety of equipment to work with, though he'd seen it listed in Tom's catalogue. "This is a really *neat* press," he remarked. "About twice as good as Tom Curtis's. That's the only one I've ever used."

"Who's Tom Curtis?" Alan asked.

"My best friend at home. You know, the one I said lives across the street from us." Briefly, Nels thought about Tom, back in Portland—maybe this minute stepping out of the Curtises' gray stucco house on the corner, looking across the street and wishing Nels were home. And for just an instant he saw exactly what Tom would be seeing—the familiar big white house with the green shutters, and that sort of chewed bush that Ruffles had ruined, and Rory's old yellow plastic scooter lying crossways of the front walk. But it was like seeing something through the wrong end of a telescope; it all seemed comfortably distant—long ago.

"You'll have news about presses for him when you go back," Alan said absently.

"Yeah," Nels murmured. But he felt as detached as Alan sounded. I won't be going back there for quite a while, he thought, almost with relief. Quite a *long* while. He smiled at how astonished Tom would be, to see where he was now—high in this airy, light-filled tower room with a really great printing press and a big worktable, and a brand new friend and a view that went on, and on.

Letting his fingers take over the job of working spacers into a couple of type slots, Nels raised his eyes to the sweep of countryside beyond the open casement. It was as good as a bird's nest, this tower—better, with no branches or leaves in your way. You could see straight to the mountains, far, pale blue humps on the horizon. And a little nearer, the dark slopes of forest patched with green and tan, slanting down into a jumble of orchards and farms and roads until the freeway sliced across with a diagonal silver-dotted line of those carbide lights. Then you could let your eye drift nearer, across more fields and farms and garden plots to the little sprawl of Reeves Ferry village, a cluster of old-fashioned dim houses and treetops . . . and right at your feet, so to speak, three stories below this window and slowly moving away, a solitary foreshortened bicycle rider with a fluff of taffy-white hair, wavering along the road beside his ink-blue morning shadow.

Stevie, heading toward his boundary line at the school playground. I still haven't written Mommie to send that insect book, Nels thought. But the accompanying pang of guilt was a mild one—once-removed, so to speak—as comfortably distant as the village spread out yonder. As if he had got his feelings into perspective too, as he never could downstairs.

He wondered how this landscape had looked in the old days, when the Inn was just Alan's family's farm. No freeway, of course; just a little country school—and maybe no paving on the road or even electric light poles. Or was that reaching too far back?

"Hey, how old is this place?" he asked Alan. "I mean, when was it a farm?"

"Hm?" Alan, rummaging in the worktable drawer, surfaced with a block of paper. "Oh. I dunno. Long time ago. I think my grandfather Reeves built the house."

"Was that the Reeves who had the ferry?" Nels asked.

"No, that was my *great*-grandfather. I think. Hey, Mom?" Alan raised his voice, turning toward the wall beyond Nels. "Was it Granddad who started the ferry?"

"No, silly, it was Dad's granddad!" came the answer, on a fluting ripple of laughter. That was *way* back. Or—wait a minute. Maybe it was Dad's great-granddad. No, I don't think so. Let me see . . ."

"Doesn't matter!" Alan shouted. To Nels, in his normal voice, he said, "It was Dad's granddad, I'm pretty sure. *My* granddad built the house. Unless I'm mixed-up, but you don't really care, do you?" Then, yelling again, "Are there any cookies or anything?"

"Not for a while. Raisin cake in the oven. I'll let you know before you actually starve to death." The light, amused voice was accompanied by the faint sounds of a drawer closing, a bowl clinking against another one, and came from beyond the wall to Nels's left, nearest the front of the building.

That's the kitchen in there, Nels told himself, trying to get a clear floor plan of the place in his mind's eye. And the living room is on *that* side, to my right. I think.

He had been in the living room only briefly, when he and Alan had gone in yesterday to hunt for more newsprint for the press. By now he was not sure which door Alan had opened, of the five that ringed the strange, dim little six-sided hall at the top of the spiral stair. On the sixth side was the stair itself, and the door directly opposite the top step was Alan's—of that much he was certain. The other four doors must open to four other slice-of-pie-shaped rooms—the living room, the kitchen . . . and there must be a bathroom and a room where Alan's parents slept. But he didn't really know.

I could find out, Nels thought. I could ask to go to the bathroom.

Impulsively he turned, his mouth already open to speak. But Alan was scribbling busily, chewing his lip the way he did when he was concentrating, and Nels turned away again. It didn't matter all that much, did it? Plenty of time. All summer. He drew a long breath, feeling that balloonman lightness again. He had never liked a friend as well as Alan, or felt more congenial with anybody.

Not that there weren't differences between them. For one thing, Alan loved to tease—that sudden whooping out the window at Stevie was typical. He loved to alarm people—Nels included—stir things up like an ant hill and watch everybody run in circles. One morning Nels had happened to mention the old General, and how Alice used to hear him jumping rope, and walking up and down. Right away Alan wanted to go down and make those noises in the General's room—give Alice a fright, maybe get everybody in the Inn all upset and believing there were ghosts. Nels had difficulty talking him out of it.

"But nobody'd ever find us—take my word!" Alan insisted.

"Maybe not, but what's the *point*?"

"Oh—just scare Alice a little—get some excitement going."

"No. We'd just make ourselves a lot of trouble. Besides, it would end up scaring the little kids, not Alice. What's the good of that?"

"Oh—!" Alan was impatient. "What's the difference if it does? Getting scared wouldn't hurt them."

"You don't know Jenny! She gets nightmares."

It was fairly obvious that Alan didn't care if she did or not, but he finally shrugged and gave up. "I just thought it would be fun."

It was the sort of thing Nels might have thought fun three or four years ago, before it had dawned on him that other people had feelings too. But he didn't say so. For the most part he and Alan liked all the same things, and the same notions struck them funny, and they grasped each other's ideas so quickly they seemed almost to be talking shorthand.

We're on the same wavelength, thought Nels comfortably, and felt he had put his finger on it.

That was the best part, the feeling of comfort, of almost lightheaded well-being, that came over him the minute he ran up those spiral stairs into the tower. No matter what had been happening downstairs, it ceased to matter here. Each morning he stood a moment looking out as he had done today, over the village and the road—often with the bright spot of Stevie's towhead wobbling along—and up ahead beyond the bicycle, the school playground with its inevitable little knot of lounging figures, one hulking one often crowded into a little kid's swing, moving idly back and forth. And it was as if they were all on some other planet—or as if *he* were, while they stayed behind on the old ordinary boring Earth. And the earlier, miserable parts of this strange spring and summer faded behind him too.

"There. That's most of it, anyhow," said Alan, throwing down his pencil. "I'll have to look some stuff up before I can finish. Have you got the titles set?"

"Long ago. Let me see it."

Alan handed him the page and tilted his chair to stretch as Nels read his article about nova stars. It was good—better than anything Nels could write. And it told a lot of stuff about novas Nels had never known, though he had read three books about astronomy—all he could find in the school library.

"Where did you find all this out?" he asked enviously.

"Oh—my dad has a book. He's got a pretty good telescope, too. Come up some night, why don't you? We can look at the Pleiades, or maybe Saturn."

"That would be *neat*," Nels said. The very idea left him

breathless—but so did the idea of trying to get away at night. "Only I don't think I could do that."

"Just wait till the others are asleep," Alan said carelessly.

But what if Stevie should wake up, and find me gone? Nels thought. He'd be scared—then everybody'd be up, and hunting for me. Oh, no, I couldn't risk that.

He was about to say so when Alan added, "Hey, do you smell raisin cake?"

Nels took a deep sniff, and was almost overcome with the fragrance of new-baked cake. At the same moment, Alan's mother's flutelike voice called from beyond the partition.

"Alan! Come and get it!"

"Be right back," Alan said, and dashed out the door.

Well, I couldn't come at night, Nels thought. But maybe I could borrow that book about astronomy. No, not borrow, but maybe I could read it up here. If his dad didn't mind . . . I've never even seen his dad. Well, I've never *seen* his mother, either, but of course I've *heard* her. She's right next door there in the kitchen. Probably she's real busy and probably his dad's always at work when I'm here. Sure, that's it.

He was wondering if the "real telescope" was just an exaggeration when Alan came back carrying two wedges of cake on fancy little plates patterned with roses like the teacups, and led the way to the old couch. The cake was wonderful—moist and golden, with a sugary, lemony crust on top instead of frosting, and studded with dark raisins. Nels had never tasted anything like it.

"Where does your dad work?" he asked between enormous bites.

"Oh—here, mostly."

"Right in this tower?"

"Well, pretty often. Sometimes he goes and works in a room at the city library, getting material and all."

"What does he do?"

"He's a sort of mathematician, and writer. I mean, he writes articles about mathematics and science and stuff for special magazines."

"He does!" Nels stopped chewing, he was so impressed.

"What does yours do?"

"He's a pilot. Not for a big airline or anything," Nels added. "He flies cargo, just to different places in the state. He and his partner."

"An air-freight line!" Alan, too, seemed interested and impressed. His dark eyes sparkled. "It's his own company, you mean?"

Nels hesitated, then said, "Yes." That's true, he told himself. Actually it's perfectly true. It's still his own. Or anyway it *will* be his own again soon.

"He's—moved it recently. It's based down in Millerton now, instead of the city."

"Oh, way down there. Hey, did he ever take you up with him? Flying?"

"Yes. A lot." Nels began to cast about for a change of subject.

"I've never even been off the ground. Not really. It must be great!"

"Yes. It *is*. It—it really is." For the life of him, Nels could think of nothing more informative to say about it, nothing calm enough to add.

Alan was silent an instant, his bright eyes on Nel's face. Then to Nels's relief he said, "Well. You finished?" and they set aside the rose-patterned plates, on which only a few golden crumbs remained, and went back to their newspaper publishing.

They were soon absorbed; it was an hour before they spoke of anything but the job at hand. Finally page three of *A.M.* was set in type and they pulled a proof—the immediate effect of which was to set them both laughing. It seemed impossible they could have scrambled so many words.

"Look at that!" said Alan, when he could speak for giggling. "Looks like a good secret cipher. *Top* secret!"

" 'Strnov arswi,' " Nels read, or attempted to. "Is that what cipher looks like?"

"Some kinds do. There's all sorts of different ones."

"I don't think I ever saw any at all."

"Really? I'll show you some if you want. I've got a whole book about 'em. It was the General's," Alan added with a grin. "I sort of borrowed it from his bookcase and never took it back."

"It was General Rutherford's?" Nels was surprised.

"Sure, he was in the Signal Corps, didn't you know that? Ciphers were his job. Hey, you want to learn some, just for fun? We could even make up one of our own! Use it to pass messages." Alan was getting excited.

Nels laughed, with some uneasiness. "Messages? From your side of the table to mine?"

"Oh, not just up here! I mean when you're downstairs. With Stevie and the others. Outdoors, even."

"No! That's too risky." Nels had been afraid he meant that, and the very idea gave his stomach the bottom-dropping-out feeling of a roller coaster. "Somebody might find one before I did. I'd have to anwer a lot of questions—"

"No you wouldn't! Dope, I'm not going to put your name on them!" Alan's eyes were dancing in a way that increased Nels's apprehension. "Nobody'd know it was meant for you—or even know what it was. It would just look like a lot of squiggles. You could play dumb—then sneak it into your pocket when nobody was looking, and decipher it later."

"But how would you get these messages to—wherever I'd find them? Downstairs and outdoors and all?"

"Oh, I didn't mean *way* downstairs," Alan said easily. "I can get them to the second floor hall, though—say right outside your bedroom door. Or outdoors on the drive, or around by the dining room—that's simple."

Yes, it would be simple enough, Nels reflected, to just throw them out various windows. But until this minute, he had assumed that Alan could not venture beyond the door of the General's room—though just why, he had never asked himself.

"How could you put one outside my door?" he blurted, then held his breath because the question was daringly direct.

Alan only made an airy gesture. "I have my methods. You'll see. It'll be fun! Now *won't* it?"

"Yes," Nels admitted. Nobody'll find them! he told himself. He was suddenly eager to start. "Yes, it will! How soon can you teach me some ciphers?"

"Right away! I think that book's in the living room. Come on, let's—" Alan broke off. The lunch bell had sounded from far below.

"I have to go," Nels muttered. His eagerness shrank like a punctured balloon, shriveled and spiraled downward into a limp nothing. It was all over for another day.

"Come back after lunch! Can't you ever?" said Alan, as they began hastily tidying the room.

"I don't know. Somebody usually needs me to—do something."

"Well, try," Alan urged him. "If not, then tomorrow morning."

"Yeah, tomorrow for sure."

"I'll find the cipher book and sort of brush up. And listen! Bring some red paper, could you? Real thin paper. Transparent."

"You mean like cellophane?"

"Yes! Red cellophane. Great!"

"What for? How much?"

"Oh, just a piece. And a red pencil or pen. I'll show you tomorrow—there's a cipher you use them for. Come on, I'd better take you down now."

As he spoke, he was leading the way out the door, across the dim little hexagonal hall, running silently down the curving stair with Nels hurrying after. It was always so fast, this part—as if once that lunch bell rang, Alan couldn't wait to get rid of him. *That's not so*, Nels told himself instantly. It's a good thing *one* of us has sense enough to hurry. If I'm late to lunch . . .

"Okay—till next time," Alan whispered, pulling open the final door. "Red cellophane. So long!"

"So long," Nels breathed. He stepped into the bookcase-closet. The light narrowed to a slit behind him, vanished as his groping hands touched the coat hook. Carefully he pushed the bookcase open a crack and listened, as always. Below, muted by floor and walls, he heard the back door slam, the little kids' voices and scrambling feet, Alice talking to them. But on this floor, silence.

He opened the bookcase, slipped out, leaned against it until he heard the muffled *click*. Immediately—as always—he was conscious of a feeling of uneasiness, of sudden depression, of an impulse to go right back in, for fear it might not be there next time he came. Also as always, he realized he had again forgotten to notice what the room was like—the one directly behind the bookcase closet. Sometimes, as he stood here like this he could not even be sure he had been there today, could not remember actually passing through the closet—although he had certainly been with Alan.

Tomorrow I'll notice that room for sure.

There was nobody on the second floor at all. Silently he ran the length of the shadowy, high hall, and into the west wing bathroom.

Five minutes later he was ambling down the stairs and along the main hall to lunch.

STEVIE, sagging disjointedly behind his chair with the weight of another interminable, boring morning making his very bones feel heavy—even my *fingernails* feel heavy, he thought, even my *ears*—watched the doorway and waited for Nels to appear in it. Sooner or later he always did appear, though where he came from, where he vanished after breakfast lately, was beyond Stevie. You could at least find him in the afternoons—even if he did seem more absentminded than ever, and less sociable, and mostly just wanting to read. But in the mornings you could yell your head off, hunting for him, and he never even heard you, though he always heard the lunch bell. Or maybe he just got hungry. Oh, no, not Nels, Stevie thought. More likely he just looked at his watch and knew it was time. Stevie's stomach told *him*, loud and clear; no need for him to look at his watch. Not that he had one. The Mickey Mouse he'd got when he was six hadn't worked for a long time. He was supposed to get a real one next month, on his tenth birthday, as Nels had. But the way things were this summer, he doubted if anybody'd remember that. It was a pretty weird summer. He wasn't even sure anybody would remember the *birthday*. Well, Nels would, of course. *And Mommie will*, said a voice inside him. But right away another interior voice, a newer one, whispered, *How do you know? She forgets our letter sometimes. She forgot to send the insect book*—that is, if Nels ever wrote her, Stevie added to himself.

"Gol, where *is* everybody?" he said loudly, sagging the other way over his chair back.

"Here we are!" Rory caroled. "Everybody's right here in front of you."

"Everybody that counts, anyhow. Eh, Teddy bear?" Alice added, reaching past him to put the sugar bowl on the table, and flipping his nose lightly as she withdrew her hand.

"Sure! Me and Jenny! We're everybody. And Steve. And Jenny. And me. And—"

Predictably, Jenny giggled and joined in. "And Alice. And Rory. And Stevie. And me. And—"

"Oh, *gol*," Stevie groaned. "Now you've got them started."

"And all the rest," said Rory brilliantly, "of our Statewide family. We here at Statewide Bankentruss welcome you, Small Businessman, key element of our basic ecominy—"

"*Economy*," said Stevie, trying not to grin. He heard that same commercial every Saturday, waiting for *Skywanderers* to start, and Rory could imitate the man's high-pitched voice exactly.

"—and our sacred trust!" Rory's voice flowed on, heedless of interruption. "Your continuing possperity is our v'dusherry responsibility, and your patternidge our pleasure! Thank - you - Small - Businessman! . . . He's a real, *real* small businessman, see him, Jenny? Standing right over there by my water glass, sort of in the shade. It's really hard to see him unless you know where to look, he's only about this high—" Carefully Rory held his finger about two inches above the tablecloth. "Glad to *see* you, Small Businessman, would you care for a bowl of soup when I get some or would you ruther—"

Jenny was falling around limp with laughter by this time and Stevie no longer resisting a reluctant, lopsided grin—just because Rory could talk so fast and so continuously, pouring out words in that airy, soaring tone of voice like a babbling brook or something without stopping to breathe or say "uh" or even think where the next weird idea was coming from. And he could keep it up as long as Jenny—or anybody—would keep on laughing.

"Well, well!" Alice's humorous-waspish voice suddenly dammed the flow. "How-do, stranger! And where were *you* when I wanted the trash carried out this morning?"

Stevie swung around to see Nels walking into the room. Instantly the day got better, and his bones less heavy. "Hey, Nels!" he said with relief, then stopped because Alice was still there by the kitchen door, still tossing some jibe or other at Nels in her discomforting way. But Nels didn't hear her, and she went on into the kitchen. So that for *you*, old Smarty Alice, Stevie thought. "Hey, Nels!" he said. "Where you been? Hey, did you write Mommie yet for that book?"

But Nels didn't answer him either—still just acted as if he didn't hear, or was thinking hard about something. And by now he was standing behind his chair, right beside Stevie.

"Hey, *Nels*," said Stevie, staring, and tugged his sleeve.

"What?" Nels said, looking around—as if he *hadn't* heard before.

"Are you *deef*?" Stevie demanded. "I said, have you written Mommie about that book?"

"Oh. No, I—forgot to. I haven't had time yet. I will, though."

"Gol! *When* will you? You been saying that for a month!"

"It's only been about a week since you first asked me."

It had been fully two, but Stevie let it pass. "Well, anyway, will you write her, please? Today? Right after lunch?"

Nels frowned slightly, but then looked away, murmuring, "Oh, okay."

He wasn't looking *at* anything in particular, just sort of out the window. The frown had passed; he didn't seem annoyed, not even exactly bored, or impatient, or—anything else Stevie could put a name to. Maybe he's sleepy, Stevie thought. He said, "You been taking a nap or something?"

No answer, no reaction at all; Nels just kept on looking thoughtfully out the window—though there was nothing to see but the scraggly inner branches of the big fir, and the front walk and store wing beyond. Stevie's puzzled gaze moved across the table. Rory and Jenny were staring too. Rory's eyes were as wide open as they would go, his fair eyebrows high above them, his dimple coming and going uncertainly.

"He's taking a nap *now*," he said. "Standing up. Boy, I didn't know anybody but horses could do that. Small Businessman, can you do that? It is your v'dusherry responsibility—"

"Shhh! Here they come," Stevie said, as much to cut off his own sudden attack of giggles as to silence Jenny's and Rory's. As the tap-shuffle of the uncle's and aunt's slow approach sounded in the hall, they stood, staring at Nels, the three of them, bursting with held-back laughter, trying not to look at each other but doing it anyway, then having to stifle their giggles again. *What's so funny?* Stevie asked himself suddenly, but he went on giggling.

At least the performance jarred Nels out of his trance. He glanced around at them and said, "Shhh!" with almost his usual older-brother sort of frown. "Why are you all acting so dumb?"

"We're not acting dumb, *you* are," Stevie muttered, feeling his grin drag down but half laughing still.

"He's awake! He's alive! Superhorse wakes from his nap, refreshed and ready for the fray!" exclaimed Rory irrepressibly, sending Jenny into new gales. In fact, she threw back her head, squeezed her eyes shut, and laughed so hard her shoulders shook and her face turned bright pink.

She's *trying* to do that, Stevie thought, watching half fascinated, half uneasy. He wished she wouldn't. Not so *hard*. It was time Nels made her quit. But Nels was just standing there again, just *standing*, as if it wasn't even happening. "Hey, Jen, quit!" Stevie began uncertainly, then looked at Nels again hoping he'd wake up and take over, as he should.

And suddenly he did, saying, "Jenny, come *on*. You'll get the hiccups." And Jenny opened her eyes and let the laughter trail off, just as the uncle and aunt arrived at last in the doorway.

"Well, here we all are again!" Aunt Ruth's brisk voice started the formula. "Hands all washed, are they? Use the soap? Hang the towel up?" . . . eyes checking the pill bottles, the window blinds, the table setting. "Well, let's sit down, then, All right, Alice!"

Stevie collapsed thankfully in his chair as Alice popped out of the kitchen door like a cuckoo from its clock, and began to serve the soup. At least they could eat, now. And after lunch maybe Nels—"Hey, Nels?" Stevie whispered, nudging him. "Nels? Want to play racing cars after lunch? I'll let you use my Ferrari. Or we can play Monopoly if you'd rather."

"Yeah, okay," Nels said, which might mean either one game or the other, but at least meant "yes" instead of "no" and sounded normal and awake.

So *then*, Stevie told himself, maybe the day would settle down and start being worth something.

ALL THROUGH LUNCH, questions kept gathering in Nels's mind like a flock of jumpy little birds—questions that never occurred to him when he was actually with Alan, or if they did, fluttered away again before he got a good look at them. Now suddenly they all came home to roost. There were bound to be answers—some good scientific explanation for everything behind that bookcase door—and he was beginning to need to find them. When the meal was over and Stevie had run upstairs to collect his racing cars, Nels seized the few free moments to drift into the kitchen as if by accident.

Alice, on her way to the sink with some plates, stopped short and widened her eyes at him. "Well, well, look who's slumming! I haven't seen you to speak to for a coon's age!"

"What d'you mean? You see me three times a day at meals."

"I said to speak to." Alice went on to the sink. "For a while there, seemed like I couldn't get my work done for falling over you and answering nine hundred and thirty-seven questions a minute. Lately you're the little man who wasn't there." She spoke with no more than her usual amused mockery, but the scrutiny she gave him over her shoulder made him feel she had turned a science fiction ray gun on him. "Where you keeping yourself these days?" she added.

"Oh, just around." Nels improvised rapidly. "I—found some books I'd never read. And I've been trying to make a sort of plan of the Inn, too. As it used to be. I'm interested in architecture."

"I see." Alice was running dishwater now, and no longer watching him. "So now you've got more questions. Ask away."

"Well, one thing, I was wondering when the Inn was first built. I mean—about what year?"

"First built," Alice mused, raising her gaze from the soapsuds and fixing it out the window. "Now I used to know that. 1898, was it? Maybe 1900."

"Nineteen hundred!" That was a *long* time ago. "Was the ferry here then?"

"Oh, long before. That thing was pre-Civil War, child. The

Inn's big heyday was along after World War I. The Twenties. Tell you what—take a look at some of those old photographs they got around here, in the halls. That'll give you an idea. Celebrities staying here! Governor of the state! Once a Senator and his family! Oh, we were something, in those days. Long before *my* time, of course."

Nels was beginning to feel tingly, as if he were on the trail of some idea that might turn out to be just great. "Well—about when was the house remodeled into an inn, d'you know?" As Alice looked puzzled, he added, "I thought—somebody told me it was just a big house, at first."

"Not that I ever heard of," Alice said blankly. "Which part was the original house, did they say?"

"This part. The whole east wing."

Alice glanced around the room, then squinted toward the ceiling. "Kitchen, pantry, dining room—and up above, the General's room and probably a couple they blocked off. That's all there is to the east wing. Where was the original living room supposed to be?"

"I don't know," Nels faltered. It was as if he suddenly felt the quiver of quicksand underfoot. Where could it have been? And what about the original front entrance? "But you *said* it was remodeled!" he burst out. "You told me that yourself!"

"Well, sure!" Alice turned to stare at him. "Nineteen sixty or so, that was—they had the whole place on its ear around here, fixing up that store in the main lounge, and the Websters' apartment up over it, and the Realty offices in yonder—"

"Oh, *that* remodeling!"

"Only one I know of. What in creation you so upset about?"

"I'm not upset, I was only . . ." Nels let the rest trail off. Glancing around for a means of escape, he saw the tray of silverware she had finished drying, and hastily offered to carry it to the pantry for her on his way out.

From the pantry he slipped through the swinging door into the empty dining room. At once, standing in the huge, shadowy room—it still smelled of ham and cucumbers—he felt easier. *Here* was the living room of the original house, and its dining room as well. Plenty of room for both. And *there* was the old front entrance, where the big sliding doors were now. He walked through them into the main hall, his step light with relief. It was all just as Alan had told him. There had been a much earlier remodeling, that was all—one Alice knew nothing about. He was never going to ask her anything again. She only confused him. It almost seemed as if she *tried* to. Maybe Stevie had been right about her all along.

Go back to the part about 1900, Nels ordered himself. *That* idea was full of promise. Alan had been sure—unless he was mixed-up—that his grandfather had built the house. Which means, Nels told himself with the tingling beginning again at the back of his neck, that his grandfather was a grown man already in 1900 . . . I don't think *my* grandfather was even born then! Well, I know he wasn't—he was young enough to be drafted in World War II. So why does Alan seem just my age? He ought to be nearer Dad's! . . . or am I mixed-up now? Why can't I get it straight? It's weird. And why don't I ever see his father, or his mother either, though I hear her talking? Are they all—*ghosts* or something?

Nels found himself standing in front of one of the groups of old photographs, looking at the flat straw hats and funny dresses, and remembering the one upstairs of the boy sitting on the folded-back top of the old car—while all the science fiction books he had ever read, the books about time-displacement and future-past, swirled through his mind in a scintillating stream.

Only I don't believe in ghosts, he thought. Anyhow not the kind in white sheets.

But what if there were other kinds of ghosts? Displaced persons, sort of?

We're all leftovers in this house, don't you know that? He could hear Alice saying it, that first day they'd come. She'd only been mocking herself, he knew. But suppose there really were leftover people here—former guests, even the original owners—stranded in walled-off rooms . . . or maybe a whole leftover pocket of *time*, captured and held in that tower, though long gone from everyplace else. Now *that* was a good scientific theory. It could be, couldn't it? Nels thought. Maybe on Alan's side of the bookcase it's still . . . he caught his breath . . . it's still thirty years ago. And on my side it's already *now*. And I'm the only one in the world who can go back and forth.

Oh, *yes*, I want it that way. Because that would be absolutely fantastically *great*.

A feeling of exhilaration rushed up through Nels, a sensation of lightness, of energy, of power. Of course one should test the theory, go at it scientifically. Alan's clothes, for instance. If the theory was right, they'd look old-fashioned—like the ones in the photographs. So far, he'd never paid much attention to Alan's clothes, beyond noticing something red. But next time I will, he resolved. Next time I'll stare.

He became aware of a persistent little husky voice at his left elbow, and looked down into Jenny's upturned face.

"Why won't you *answer*?" she said. "I been yelling and yelling and yelling and yelling and—"

He managed to break through and say he was sorry, and ask what she wanted, and she quit being outraged and began to tell him, but he had trouble keeping his mind on what she was saying. "Read to you? You mean now? Well, I can't now, Jenny," he said gently, remembering he'd promised to play racing cars with Stevie, and beginning to feel burdened and helpless again. "Maybe this evening—"

"Nels?" said Jenny in an odd, soft little voice.

"What?"

"How come you never read to me any more?"

She was staring up at him, eyes sad and puzzled in her round little face—wide eyes, like a kitten's, slightly tilted at the outer corners, and the same color as the tawny bangs that hung halfway down over them. Her hair needs trimming—needs *combing*, Nels thought with a pang that was half pity, half stabbing guilt. Nobody takes care of her right anymore. Nobody even pays attention. "Jenny, shall I comb your hair?" he offered.

"*No*!" Jenny cried indignantly, shrinking back and wrapping both arms over her head.

At the very moment he was realizing how stupid *that* had been, he noticed what she was holding: in one hand, a strawberry sucker, the kind they sold in the store, and in the other hand the red cellophane she had just peeled off it. "Oh! May I have that?" he exclaimed, reaching for the cellophane.

She gave a little scream of exasperation, flung the paper at him, and stalked off toward the main stairs. Before he could call her back he heard the clatter of Stevie's shoes on the stair, and his loud, relieved, "Well, I finally found my Ferrari! In Rory's drawer!"

Before he knew what he meant to do, Nels spun around, ran silently along the back passage, and then took the back stairs on tiptoe three at a time, his cellophane clutched in his hand. At the top he hesitated, a confused welter of emotions and second thoughts and impulses and dismay and remorse all battling within him. As he stood there, his eyes fell on the group of old photographs between the tall windows—and one urgent need abruptly dominated the rest. In a moment he was there, peering eagerly at the boy perched on the folded top of the old car.

And it was Alan to the life.

THAT WAS the first day Nels disappeared right after lunch, the same way he did after breakfast every morning. At first Stevie couldn't believe it, and spent ten or fifteen minutes hunting for him—checked the store, and even went out the front entrance and stood on the flagstone path to peer around. But Nels was just—gone. Just while I was finding my racers, Stevie thought, slowly stuffing the two tiny cars in his pocket. He wished he'd settled for Monopoly—he could have got the game from the bay window cupboard without letting Nels out of his sight. How can he do it so *fast*? he thought. Where does he go?

There was nobody on the road, except a big boy, on foot, coming from the direction of the river and probably headed for the store. Stevie walked around the curve of the dining room and down the graveled drive toward the back of the Inn, looking every which way, even through the gate into the service yard. Nels's bike was still there, beside his own, in the rack near the back steps. Jenny came out the door just then, carrying her largest and most dilapidated stuffed bear, and licking a strawberry sucker.

"You see Nels?" Stevie asked her.

"A little while ago I did. He took my cellophane."

"He what?"

"Took my cellophane wrapper that was around my sucker. And now I can't lay it down in case I want to, I'll have to eat it all at once. And I don't like to eat them all at once. I'd ruther—"

"Hey, Jen, listen. Where'd he go after you saw him? Did you notice?"

"No, I just asked him if he'd read to me, because Rory wants to watch that yucky cartoon before we go to Maureen's, but he wouldn't, and only wanted to comb my *hair*, and then he said, 'Oh, can I have that?' and took my cellophane and so I just ran away. Stevie?"

"What?"

"What's the *matter* with Nels? He acts funny."

"I know," Stevie said uneasily. "Where was this? I mean where were you when you talked to him?"

"Right outside the dining room."

"And you didn't see where he went?"

"No. He never reads to me any more," Jenny said fretfully. "Good-bye, I'm going to Maureen's." She started for the driveway.

"Your bear's dragging. His foot is. Hold him up a little higher," Stevie told her.

Jenny just said, "He doesn't mind," and kept going, busy again with her sucker.

Stevie heaved a sigh and started in the other direction, wandering out the west end of the service yard past the Rooftop Realty and Insurance, glancing in the open door just in case, but seeing nobody but the secretary, Doris Somebody, the one with the bright orange hair, pecking away at her typewriter.

At the rear of the Inn, he stood a moment staring speculatively across the weed-grown rose garden to the tangle of lilacs and trees rising jungle-thick behind it. There was another road back there somewhere—it curved around toward town and became a paved street, the one the church stood on. Nels *might* go through here, to see somebody who lived on that other road. Somebody Stevie didn't know. It was possible. Though not very.

But if he didn't go somewhere *out* of the Inn, it left only one possibility: he was still *in* the Inn. And that meant deliberately hiding.

Okay, Stevie told himself, turning on his heel. So he doesn't want to play with me. Or *be* with me. So okay! Who cares? Nobody's going to hang around his neck.

That's what his mother had especially advised him not to do, when Nels first started being—well, hard to find now and then, or crabby—way along last spring. "Don't hang around his neck, Stevie. Don't *badger*. Let him alone sometimes, everybody needs that. Remember, he's twelve. He's probably already spinning some sort of private teen-age cocoon—and I grant you they can be mighty knobby, unattractive affairs, too. But it won't last forever. And you watch—a beautiful butterfly might emerge one day."

"Not from a cocoon," Stevie couldn't help saying.

"What?"

"Only moths emerge from cocoons. Butterflies make chrysalises."

His mother closed her eyes briefly, then opened them. "Chrysalis, then. But you catch my meaning?"

"Yeah. Don't badger," Stevie said.

So he would not badger, or hang around Nels's neck. Let Nels hide under the bed or somewhere all day long if that's what he wanted to do. Stevie would go ask Uncle Fred for a box to make a beetle cage.

He went into the main hall from the rear, through the French doors, and caught sight of the mail spread out on the long table at the foot of the stairs. Quickly he went to look over it. Only stuff for the Rooftop Realty and a boring-looking magazine for Uncle Fred. No cards from Dad, and it wasn't the right day yet for his mother's letter. He took the magazine and went on into the store, and over to the cash register.

"Well, howdy-do, young man. Oh, the mail came, did it? Thankee, thankee."

"You're welcome," Stevie said, "Hey, Uncle Fred—"

Before he could get any farther, the high school boy he had seen earlier stepped up to the cash register to pay for whatever he'd bought. Stevie turned away quickly, pretending to be interested in oranges and lemons.

"That's okay, kid, you were first," the boy said.

"Oh, I—no, I—wasn't buying anything," Stevie mumbled.

"That's just my grandnephew," Uncle Fred put in as he began peering through his glasses at Aunt Ruth's penciled sales slip, then peering over them as he slowly punched this key, then that one, then another one, on the cash register. "Staying with us for a spell, him and his brothers and sister. Nice bunch of children." The cash drawer burst open with a ringing jangle of sound. "That's three seventy-five, Ernie, according to my magical machine. Yep, this young man and I are pretty good friends, aren't we, Old Timer?" Uncle Fred gave his usual little grin and nod at Stevie, then added to Ernie, "Comes in here and talks away to me, ninety to nothing, as if he and I were about the same age. How's your father, Ernie? Leg any better?"

The boy answered something, and Stevie slipped outside, hot with embarrassment and wishing grown-ups wouldn't talk about you when you were standing right *there*. He moved around to the other side of the big scraggly rhododendron by the steps, wondering if he could get another look at the boy's fancy belt buckle when he came out, without being especially noticeable himself. It was a great big silverish buckle, with a sort of emblem. Only he hadn't quite seen what the emblem was.

In a minute he heard the screen door bang, and the boy—Ernie—came down the steps carrying his grocery sack. Stevie stood motionless beside the rhododendron, attempting to merge with his background like a beetle, while he squinted hard at the buckle. It was a—it was something like a . . . It was a *skull*. With a rattlesnake coiled around it. You could see the little rattles on the tip of the tail.

"Gol!" said Stevie, forgetting he was going to be inconspicuous. He glanced up and found the boy standing there looking right at him. "That's a neat belt buckle," he mumbled.

"Thanks," Ernie said, and smiled a little. "Glad you like it."

"Where'd you get it?"

"Oh, a bunch of us ordered them from this catalogue. For a bike club we belong to."

"Bike club!" Stevie was suddenly buoyant with hope. "I didn't know they had bike clubs. I've got a bike, I ride it all the time. Do they let—"

"Not that kind of bike, kid," Ernie told him. "Motorbikes. Hey, I've seen you riding your bike, I think—up along by the schoolgrounds. Mornings. What's your name?"

Stevie told him.

"Where you from, Portland? What d'you think of our little burg?"

"It's okay, I guess."

"But pretty dead, huh? Yeah, you're right. Well, gotta get this stuff home." He gave a sort of salute, and turned away.

"Where do you live?" Stevie asked him.

"Down there a ways." Ernie gave a jerk of his head. "By the old ferry landing." He started across the weed-grown gravel in the direction of the river.

Stevie ran after him. "Hey. Did you—when you were coming, did you see a blond kid? On the road or anywhere? Twelve years old?"

"Afraid not. Sorry." Ernie kept on walking.

Stevie watched his stocky figure—broad, flat back, ragged brown hair, thick-muscled arm holding the grocery sack—until a clump of trees hid him. He looked really strong, almost like a person's dad. Stevie bet he was a good swimmer. He lived right by the river, too. That would really be neat. If a person got to know him a little better, he might—just might—teach a person how to swim.

Only probably not, Stevie told himself realistically.

But anyway, Ernie was pretty nice. Maybe those other big guys were nice, too. How do I know? Stevie thought. Maybe I could go play on the swings and things all day, and they wouldn't care at all. Or even get to know them. I could at least go once, and find out.

Not right now, though. But he really would, some other time. When he felt like it.

Stevie went back in the store to ask Uncle Fred for his box.

NOT TILL he was edging behind the carved screen did it occur to Nels that Alan might not be expecting him back till morning. But Alan was waiting, with a welcoming grin, and a satisfied, "Good! I knew you'd come."

"I don't see how!" Nels marveled as they headed for the bookcase. "I didn't know it myself till—"

"Careful—that latch. Oh, it was just a hunch, I guess. Did you find any cellophane?"

"Yes! But only by pure luck." Nels dug in his pocket for the sucker wrapper. "Will this do?"

"Great! I found a red pencil myself. Now I'll show you something." As they reached his room, Alan made straight for the worktable and tore off a sheet of scratch paper. Nels, glancing out the window as he waited, saw Jenny walking alone down the driveway, lugging her most beloved stuffed bear and working on her sucker. At once he had to push back the tangle of uneasy regrets that began to squirm about in him like a sackful of octopuses. I *will* read to her tonight, for sure, he told himself, and felt easier, though his gaze lingered on her until the corner of the house hid her from view.

"You aren't watching," Alan complained.

Quickly Nels turned his attention to the scratch paper. Alan had written—with an ordinary pencil, very lightly—*Danger. Spies around. Destroy all evidence*. Now, with the red pencil, he boldly lettered right over this, *Gone to grocery store, back in fifteen minutes*—obliterating the first message. As Nels opened his mouth to ask the point of that, Alan slipped the cellophane over the paper. Instantly, the bold red lettering vanished—just vanished completely—leaving the penciled message clearly revealed.

Nels could not help exclaiming, "That's *neat*. Like magic!"

"Isn't it?" Alan sounded as proud as if he'd invented it himself. "I've got two others to show you, too—the Pigpen and the Rosicrucian. Here, sit down and try the red one yourself, while I draw some little diagrams."

The magic worked as well for Nels as it had for Alan, which proved, of course, that it wasn't magic at all, but merely a natural phenomenon with a logical scientific explanation, same as everything else—perfectly logical once you'd found it. Like the explanation for the tower, Nels told himself, and suddenly remembered to look hard at Alan's clothes.

But after all, he saw nothing to prove or disprove his leftover-pocket-of-time theory. Alan's haircut seemed neither old-fashioned nor new-fashioned, just shaggily in need of a trim, like his own. The shirt was just a shirt, the something red, a sleeveless scarlet sweater—both dateless. The pants did seem different—more the sort in the old photographs, though that one in the hall was so faded you really couldn't tell what the boy was wearing. And his tennis shoes were higher-topped than Nels's.

Still, for all Nels knew, such pants and shoes were regular school clothes in Reeves Ferry.

"What's the matter? My slip show?"

Nels glanced up quickly and encountered Alan's mischievous dark eyes. "No, but your shoe's untied," Nels said casually, and turned away thinking, *he* knows what's going on, he knows all about it, he just won't tell me.

And he didn't quite dare ask. Better never to solve the puzzle than to ruin everything. Sooner or later he'd find all the pieces, then the picture would be complete.

"There," Alan said, throwing down his pencil. "Now look at this thing. It's like a tic-tac-toe diagram, sort of—only with six spaces instead of four, see, and you write ABC in the first space, and EFG in the middle one . . ."

Nels bent over the diagram with him, put his mind to the explanation of it, and gradually began to lose interest in searching for pieces to the Alan puzzle. Ciphers were more fun.

IV

GINGERBREAD DAY

NELS NEVER did mention not showing up that day to play racing cars, though Stevie waited the rest of the week for him to say something, anything, about it. He seemed simply to have forgotten he'd promised. Or else just wanted Stevie to get the message, loud and clear. That first day—it was a Monday—he didn't turn up again until four o'clock. (Naturally, thought Stevie at the time. Just what you'd expect of a Monday.) But Tuesday it was the same—a brief appearence at lunchtime, then gone until four. On Wednesday, it was almost five. And not a word about it—as if the rest of them didn't exist.

Okay, then. Just so I know, Stevie told himself doggedly. Nobody's going to badger anybody, I just want to get it straight, that's all.

By Thursday he was beginning to get it very straight. Clearly, this was how things were going to be now—how Nels wanted them. Thursday morning, he didn't even want to have a casual conversation while they dressed. Stevie asked a perfectly ordinary question—something about their dad's phone call the night before—and Nels acted like a threatened turtle, pulled right into his shell, wouldn't even tell Stevie what was wrong, just said nothing was. Well, something was. In Stevie's opinion, everything was.

Even so, after breakfast he checked in their room as always, just to make really sure Nels was gone again, before he wandered on downstairs and into the store, trying not to think how many hours had to pass till evening.

Right away, like a fingernail on the blackboard, Uncle Fred

started talking about that phone call too—as if it was something great or something.

"Well, I hear I missed an event, turning in so early. What'd your dad have to say for himself?"

"Oh—nothing." Dad never said anything on the telephone, really—none of them did. How could you say anything that mattered, when you couldn't even look at the person?

"Getting along well, is he?"

"I guess so." At least he'd *sounded* okay. Stevie made an effort and dredged up a tidbit for Uncle Fred. "He said he'd be flying right over here regular, for about a week. In the afternoons. He said he'd buzz us."

"Well! Now that'll be something to look forward to. Expect you all miss him, don't you? Your big brother—he was looking pretty downhearted at breakfast, I thought. Felt sorry for him."

Stevie didn't comment. He didn't want to talk about Nels. Or about Dad, either. "Uncle Fred," he broke in hurriedly. "Do you have anything you want me to do? In the store? You know, to sort of help around? Maybe stack up oranges, or stuff like that. Sweep the floor. I can sweep real good."

"Oh, we'll holler if we need you, we surely will." Uncle Fred chuckled in an absent-minded way, opening paper-wrapped rolls of nickels and dimes for the cash register. "You can amuse yourself any way you like, Old Timer—long as you don't get in your aunt's way."

"But couldn't I really do something? I could wait on people. I know where things are. Or anyway, I could put things in sacks for them, or . . ." Stevie glanced around the store in search of inspiration, found none, and turned back pleadingly to Uncle Fred. "I don't have anything to *do,*" he explained.

"What, with all this nice sunshine we've been getting? Me oh my, I wish I could be outdoors in it, running around and playing." Uncle Fred peered dreamily through the dusty front windows to the patches of road and trees visible between rising pyramids of canned soup and dangling ads for soapflakes.

Grown people, Stevie had noticed, invariably talked about "running around and playing" as if the two meant the same thing. When there was nothing to play and no one to play with, who wanted to just "run around"? Well, Uncle Fred would, he supposed, feeling a twinge of sympathy, or anybody who couldn't run at all, but that wasn't really the point just *now*. "I'm tired of sunshine!" he said. "I'd rather work at something. Couldn't I wash those windows?"

Uncle Fred laughed outright at this, but reached a long arm to pat Stevie's shoulder as he did so. "Ruth?" he called. "Here's a boy so tired of sunshine he's willing to wash windows. What say, got a little odd job or two to keep him out of mischief?"

"Oh, my conscience, I don't know." At the rear of the store, Aunt Ruth straightened from a half-empty canned goods shelf. "I guess he could take this carton to the trash for me. Just put it in the storeroom, Stevie. And you can drag a full one in. It'll say Bertrand's Spiced Peaches on the side."

"Okay," Stevie said eagerly, dashing for the storeroom.

"Here—here—take the empty," called Aunt Ruth.

"Oh, yeah." Stevie dashed back, grabbed the carton from her, swung around barely avoiding a stack of cornflake boxes, which teetered perilously, and hurried to the storeroom with Aunt Ruth's "Slower, *slower*!" following him.

He was busy a full half-hour, trotting back and forth between the storeroom and the shelf, feeling useful and employed. But by ten o'clock the shelf was replenished, and as for the floor, Aunt Ruth had swept it earlier.

"The front window's dirty," Stevie reminded her.

"No, no, child, I can't have you climbing around on ladders, you'd likely break your neck. If you really want to help me, just go along outdoors somewhere and play."

So there he was on his own again, wandering about in front of the Inn, alternately watching for beetles in the patchy grass and staring more and more thoughtfully up the road to the school. After a while he got his bike and pedaled up there slowly, cutting his eyes around to watch the big boys idling in the playground, counting them, identifying Ernie standing over beside the swings, then pedaling slowly back to the Inn. It might be sort of uncomfortable, getting to know them. Or even impossible. But he was going to try—and soon.

I'll go tomorrow, Stevie resolved.

But the following morning—it was Friday—he came out of the bathroom to see Rory just swinging around the newel-post and scampering down the stairs, and when he went on into his and Nels's room, to his utter astonishment Nels was *there*, sitting at the desk big as life.

"Hi!" Stevie said joyfully. And suddenly it wasn't astonishing at all that Nels was there, but just ordinary and *right*. Maybe he'd been wrong about Nels avoiding him. Maybe the all-day absences were over now, maybe the whole thing was over, the vanishing after breakfast, everything—behind them both forever. It wasn't so bad, Stevie thought, tremulous with relief, as he felt the world go back to normal. Friday! He might have known it would end on a Friday. He came on toward the desk, saying, "Whatcha doing?"

"Nothing," Nels said. He got up quickly, pushed something into a drawer, tried to stuff a long thin strip of paper or something into his pocket. It looked funny, dangling and wiggling there, like a paper snake.

"What *is* that thing?" Stevie asked him, reaching for it.

"*Nothing*, I said!" Nels fended him off, backed up against the desk. He looked angry, Stevie saw now—flustered, almost scared. "Quit grabbing, can't you?"

"Okay, okay, I don't want your precious whatsit." Stevie backed away, waving his arms.

Nels said, "Where's Rory? Isn't he still . . . I thought he—"

"He went downstairs. Hey, you want to play something? Or go outdoors?"

"Oh—not now." Nels turned his back, opened a desk drawer, shut it again, moved some papers.

"We could go to Parker's meadow. I finally got a real good box from Uncle Fred, or not a box, a styrofoam thing that jelly jars came in, and it's got all these little compartments, and if we put screen or something across the top, why—"

"No, I don't *want* to. You go ahead."

"But it's for a beetle cage! Wouldn't that be neat? We could keep 'em alive, and then when we get the insect book—Hey, did you write Mommie for the book yet?"

Nels whirled around at him. "*No*, I did not write Mommie for the book yet!" he almost yelled. "Boy, I wish you'd quit nagging and nagging about that book! Why don't you write her yourself, you can write, can't you? You're not illiterate, are you? Boy! If I hear about that book just one more time, I'll just about . . ."

He let the rest trail off, turned away again. Stevie said nothing. He couldn't. He felt stunned, as if Nels had suddenly clubbed him.

"Well, it's not my fault," Nels muttered. "You keep at me, and at me . . . anyway, you ought to *practice* writing letters, then you wouldn't think it was so much work. I'll write her now, this minute," he said in a rude, angry voice, as if he didn't even care how Stevie felt.

"You don't need to," Stevie managed to say. "I'll do it. I *would've*, only you said you were going to, but—"

"No, I'll *do* it." Nels was yanking paper out of the drawer, scrabbling for a pencil. "I did say I would," he added more calmly. "I really meant to, I just kept forgetting." He sat down at the desk, rapidly began scrawling the letter.

"That's okay," Stevie mumbled. He moved over to the window and stood there without moving or saying a word until Nels had crammed the letter into an envelope and addressed it and found a stamp.

"There!" Nels said. He stood up, shoved the letter at Stevie. "Take it down right now and put it on the mail table, and it'll go out today. Go on, hurry!" he added before Stevie could even say thanks.

Stevie went down the stairs, encased in a hot balloon of humiliation, overwhelmingly aware that he had badgered, and hung around Nels's neck, that he should have written the letter himself, that nothing was back to normal at all, but everything was worse.

Of course, by the time he got back up to their room again, Nels was gone. Vanished as if he'd never been there.

So Stevie rode his bike to the school grounds after all—following a visit to the store that got him nothing but a package of lemon drops and firm dismissal.

The big boys were there, six or eight of them lounging around on the swings or bars, or tinkering with somebody's motor scooter. Stevie could see Ernie's shaggy brown head, along with some others, bent over the machine. This time, instead of just riding a few slow figure-eights in the road and then poking back to the Inn again as he had always done before, he turned in at the school driveway. Thoughtfully sucking at a lemon drop, he pedaled once around the circle and out to the road again, then back in and once around the parking lot—then finally clear around behind the school, and onto the playground from that edge.

Of course by that time they were all watching, waiting for him to appear from someplace. Stevie wasn't sure himself whether he'd been trying to avoid attention or attract it, but he'd attracted it, all right, and the minute he and his bike popped out from behind the corner of the school, there was a burst of guffaws and comments.

"There he is! Never fell in, after all!"

"Well, look what jumped out from under that *ce*-ment block."

"Hey, Cottontop, let's see you do it in reverse, now!"

The ones who didn't yell anything just stared a minute and turned back to whatever they were doing. Only Ernie smiled, and gave a little wave before bending over the bike again. Stevie made a big, vague circle around the baseball diamond and ended up a lot closer to the swings, and only a dozen or so feet from Ernie. He braced one foot on the ground and said, "Hi."

Ernie glanced up again, said, "Hi, kid," and went back to his tinkering.

"Who's your friend, Ernie?" said somebody. And somebody else said, "Don't look now but there's this little green man . . ." There were a lot of other boring, unfunny remarks Stevie had fully expected and just stood there and waited out, sucking his lemon drop.

Pretty soon Ernie straightened up and said to the others, "His name's Stevie and he's from the city and he's staying down at the Inn with the Websters. He's a nephew or something. So did anybody bring a screwdriver?"

"Here, I've got one," somebody answered, and the normal conversations started again.

Then one of them, wearing a battered sort of red hat and sitting in a swing, looked around at Stevie and said, "Okay, punk, you've seen it all. Go on, buzz off. Go haunt a house or something."

Stevie looked at him but stayed where he was.

"You say something, Wally?" said one of the others with a sort of muffled laugh.

The red-hat one, Wally, scowled and said, "Shut up. How about you trying to get rid of him?"

Another one—it was the big one perched up on the jungle gym—said to Stevie, "Why don't you go on home, Shorty? What d'you want to hang around here for?"

Ernie straightened up and half turned, but before he could say anything, Stevie said, rapidly and sort of under his breath, "It's not your playground. I got as much right here as you have."

"Okay, okay!" the big one said, rolling his eyes and flinging up his hands as if somebody had a gun in his back. Several people laughed. Somebody else said, "So play! Who's stopping you?" Red-hat said, "Yeah, come on, start. What d'you want to do?"

"I want to swing," Stevie said.

Ernie still didn't say anything. Nobody said anything; there was a silence as Stevie put down his bike with a clatter that sounded louder than usual, and walked across the open space and past Ernie and some others right to the swings, and sat down on the one next to Red-hat and began to swing. He was breathing hard and feeling hot in the face and wishing he hadn't done this, but on the other hand he felt a sort of angry relief, too. Let them go ahead and beat him up or whatever they were going to do. He didn't care.

There were a couple of snickers. Somebody said, "Got any other questions, Wally?" and there was a burst of laughter. It was different, though. Stevie was swinging back and forth, teeth clenched, looking nowhere but at his own dusty sneakers with the knot in one shoelace, but he could hear the difference. Even Wally laughed a little, and took off his red hat and put it on Stevie so that it came down over his eyes. He pushed it back, but not off, and there was some more laughter and a few comments he couldn't separate from each other. Then the hat was lifted from his head and Wally left the other swing half twisting and untwisting on its chains, and walked over to talk to somebody beside the teeter-totters. Everybody just began gradually talking to each other again.

Stevie raised his eyes cautiously from his shoes and there was Ernie, standing beside the swing looking half amused and half something else, Stevie wasn't sure what.

"Okay, Stevie. Not bad for a featherweight. But you better buzz off now, don't you think so?"

"Yeah," said Stevie. He got up from the swing, automatically reached in his pocket for another lemon drop, and on second thought pulled out the package and offered it to Ernie, who took it, looking surprised. "It's okay, you can have 'em all," Stevie told him. "I can get more." He went over and climbed on his bike, and rode one more circle on the baseball diamond, then out onto the road. He glanced back at the boys as he started toward the Inn. Somebody waved and hooted—not Ernie, he was bent over the motorbike again—and Wally flapped his red hat in an exaggerated fly-swatting motion, producing a couple of yipping laughs that pushed Stevie away farther and faster than his bike was carrying him. Then it was all behind, and there was just the empty road like every other morning—and a lot of the morning still stretching blankly ahead. And he hadn't accomplished a thing, as far as he could tell, or made friends with those big kids, which was a dumb idea anyway because he probably never would.

He put his bike away and wandered across the road toward the railroad trestle, then stopped, staring drearily in the direction of the river, instead. Maybe if he walked down to the ferry landing he could figure out where Ernie lived. Only what good would that do? Maybe he should go get his styrofoam jelly jar carton and try to make the beetle cage. The trouble was he didn't know where to find some screen to fasten on top—or how to fasten such a thing to styrofoam. Netting would be better, a fine netting—and you could see through it better, to watch the beetles. Only where did you get netting? Nels always knew stuff like that. But Stevie didn't.

Sighing, he was starting toward the river, kicking a rock along in front of him, when he heard Jenny pounding up the path from Maureen's house, yelling at him to wait. When she caught up she just walked alongside him, breathing hard, then said, "Do *you* think Mommie'll send the gingerbread men?"

"What gingerbr— Oh. You mean on Gram's birthday." Stevie's thoughts scurried around a minute without getting anywhere. "I don't even remember what day that's supposed to be," he told her.

"Tomorrow, Rory says." Jenny shot a glance over her shoulder, glowering. Rory and Maureen were following, some distance back. "*He* says she won't even remember."

"Well, *I* don't know," Stevie said. "Probably she won't."

Jenny whirled on him, glared up at him with her eyes full of tears, and yelled, "She *will*!" Then she hit at him with both hands, and started running toward the Inn, crying furiously.

"Look *out*!" Stevie shouted, then muttered, "Gol!" and rolled his eyes up as she darted right across the road without a glance in either direction. Pure dumb luck there wasn't a car, he told himself. Dumb girl, it's not my fault, no use getting mad at me.

I'll bet Mommie won't remember, he thought as he started again for the ferry landing. Everything's too different this summer. If she's going to forget my birthday why would she remember any old Gingerbread Day? Anyway who wants it? It wouldn't taste the same. Nothing's the same. Nothing's any good any more.

Gol, I hate today! Stevie told himself, kicking his rock a good eight feet into the weeds. You'd think it was a Monday.

IT WAS a bad way for a morning to start, Nels felt, a bad, unlucky way. He had scarcely waited for the bright spot of Stevie's towhead to disappear down the stairwell toward the mail table before bolting up the hall as fast as he could run. But he still felt bungling and flustered, with the bad taste in his mouth of having made a mess of things. Once behind the screen into the safety of the east wing passage, he stopped, leaning against the bathroom doorjamb with closed eyes, and drawing long, uneven breaths. He hated being at odds with Stevie—with anybody, for that matter. He hated losing his temper. And he hated feeling guilty about it afterwards.

But it wasn't only that. It was the letter he'd written his mother, somehow or other. Now why should I feel guilty about *that?* Nels demanded of himself, desperately groping after reason and logic. As if I'd failed her or something. All I was doing was writing her! No use—a ripple of agitation and fresh anxiety went over him as he discovered it: just writing to his mother—that's what was bothering him. Probably why he'd been putting it off.

That, and—of course—the telephone call night before last.

Sickeningly, he found the whole thing starting up again in his brain like some remorseless tape recording—right from the beginning, from the very ring of the phone and Aunt Ruth's cheerful summons, followed by the clamor and arguing as the younger ones jostled each other for precedence, then their suddenly bashful performances, predictable as dawn: "Hi, Daddy. Fine, how are you? . . . Oh, nothing . . . I don't know . . . Um-hm . . . Well, Rory wants to talk now . . . okay, g'bye" . . . then finally his own turn, and the others straggling off down the hall as he heard his father's voice, deep and familiar and almost painfully welcome. "Hi, there, Skipper. Last in line as usual." And his own response, predictable too—"Oh, I don't mind. Well—uh. What's new?"

And then the pause—and the totally unpredictable, unexpectable reply: "There is something new. I might be leaving. Come September or around there. Blasting right out of this rut. I might just cut my losses and go."

"Go—where?" Nels had asked around the sudden constriction in his throat.

"Alaska. Pipe-line country, boy. Nowadays a bush pilot up there makes more in a week than I can make in a . . ." The voice changed, lost its hearty note. "Listen, Skip. You may remember I mentioned something once about . . . the two of us?"

"Oh. Yeah. I remember."

"Well—so how'd you like to just come along? Team up with me?"

A pause while Nels struggled with his tight throat. "You mean—move to Alaska? Clear away from—the others? To stay?"

"Well, yes. That's what I . . . We always got along pretty good, didn't we? At least, I thought so."

"Oh, *sure*. Only—I mean—" Nels could hardly speak at all. Alaska! So far—so final. "Will you be going—anyway?"

"I think so. Skip, you don't know how it is, to be this close but not *with* any of you. I don't think I can take it much longer.

I mean—there's five of you there together, or anyway will be when you're home. I've got to have *somebody*. Can you see that?"

"Oh—yes—yes, I—"

"Easy, now. Blast it, I didn't mean to get you all upset. Farthest thing from my . . . Look, Skipper. Nothing's certain about this yet. Won't know for a month. And there's no obligation. I mean I wouldn't want you to feel . . ." His father seemed to be stumbling a good bit too. "No use pretending I don't hope you'll want to stick with me, but—well, it's entirely up to you. You understand, don't you?"

"Oh, yes." All too sickeningly, Nels understood. *Entirely up to him*.

"Well. No harm in giving it some thought. Better keep it to yourself for now, though. Might not even pan out."

"Okay. I will. G'bye."

And that was all. That's *all*, Nels told himself, as the tape came mercifully to its end. No need to get so . . . nothing's certain. It might not even pan out. So quit *thinking* about it. He straightened up from the doorjamb he had been huddling against and cleared his mind, swept it clean and bare. Back into the blank rushed Stevie, and the letter to his mother, and the guilty feeling. Hastily he walked into the General's room, saw Alan turn from the window and then hesitate at sight of him.

"What's the matter?"

"Nothing, nothing. Little trouble getting away. Come on, let's go." Nels avoided Alan's eye as they hurried together up the spiral stair. All he wanted was to forget that little trouble, not discuss it.

Alan made no comment. As he opened the door to his room, he asked cheerfully, "Well, could you read it?"

"Read—? Oh, your cipher message." Nels had almost forgotten what started the trouble in the first place. "Sure, easy.

Stevie almost caught me at it, though," he couldn't help adding.

"How'd that happen?"

"Oh, I don't know. Rory was late going out. And I guess I was careless." And that tape was playing, over and over. "I about bit Stevie's head off," he said.

"Oh, well," Alan said airily.

"Well, *he* hadn't done anything," Nels retorted.

"Okay, okay, don't start on me," Alan soothed him. "I only meant, 'Oh, well, just so you made it here safe.' "

"Yeah," Nels said. But he didn't like near-misses. He didn't like any part of this morning. "We'd better not risk leaving messages down there anywhere," he said firmly. "Stevie's no dummy. One more funny-looking piece of paper lying around the place, and he's going to be onto the whole thing."

"He can't. Not possibly. Just tell me how he could possibly catch onto us. Tell me one way."

"By figuring out a cipher! What if he'd got a really good look at this?" Nels fished the long, snakelike strip of paper from his pocket, found a pencil on the table and wound the paper evenly around it. The "clear" message was now revealed along the shank of the pencil: *Honorable escape expert invited to cookie party today in humble tower*. Nels smiled a little in spite of himself—but only briefly. "It'd take Stevie about five minutes to work that out," he said.

"Only if he knew it was supposed to be a message," Alan argued. He unwound the paper and dangled it in front of Nels—a mere torn strip, showing unrelated clusters of letters along the extreme right-hand edge. But the spiral pigtail curl of the strip was still a giveaway that its secret lay in wrapping it around something exactly the size of a pencil, and Nels shook his head.

"Five minutes," he repeated.

"Well, all we need is a harder cipher," Alan said briskly. "I've got one, too. It's—"

Nels overrode him. "We need to quit taking risks. If we *had* to do it, okay. But we don't have to, and it's just—stupid!"

"Oh, come on!" Alan's voice held a note of scorn, and his smile a challenge. "What are you, chicken?"

"No, I'm not. But I'm not stupid, either!" We're quarreling, Nels thought in dismay.

"I *am*, you mean?"

"No, I don't mean that and you know it. All I mean is I don't want everything spoiled—and for no reason!"

"Who says there's no reason?"

"I say it!" Nels burst out. "You just want to bug Stevie. That's all it is. You just like to bug people!"

He glared at Alan, thinking miserably, Now I've lost my temper again, what's the matter with me this morning? and for a minute Alan just stared back, his dark eyes wary. Then his face relaxed; he turned away, shrugging impatiently, saying, "What if I do? I don't see anything so bad about that."

"Well—it isn't much fun for Stevie," Nels muttered. But his indignation suddenly began to seem exaggerated; Alan's manner was plainly telling him not to be tiresome. He took a long breath. "Anyhow, let's *forget* it and do something else. What's the new cipher?"

Alan became his cheerful self at once as he launched into a description of the new cipher, which was called the Vigenère after its inventor, and was really neat once you got the preliminary work done. "It's kind of a lot of trouble," he added apologetically. "But I think it's worth it. Maybe you won't."

"Oh, I probably will," Nels said, struggling for his usual amiability.

"Okay, sit down, first we've each got to make a kind of special chart—it's called a Vigenère Tableau." Alan took a sheaf of graph paper from the worktable drawer and began demonstrating how to make the chart, which turned out to consist of a "clear" alphabet running across the top of the page, a "key" alphabet running down the left side, then twenty-six more alphabets filling in the square, each beginning with the letter matching the one beside it in the "key."

It *was* rather a lot of trouble. But it began to have a nice professional-looking complexity about it as Nels worked his way down the page, and an order and logic amid the complexity that strongly appealed to him. This was a *real* cipher, bound to be harder than the red cellophane trick, or any they'd tried so far. Those easy ones would be great for little kids—Rory would love them—but full of risk if you had a secret you really had to keep. And I really do, Nels reflected as his pencil went on rapidly filling in alphabets. He glanced at Alan's curly head, bent over his graph paper. Why did Alan love to rile people? Even when he wasn't there to watch them react? Not just Stevie, either, Nels thought resentfully, beginning on his sixteenth alphabet. He likes to bug me, too, or he wouldn't keep getting me into these tight corners—or making me think I'm in one. Yelling out the window at Stevie, leaving cipher messages around . . . he can watch *me* react, all right, and he enjoys it.

"I beat you," he said a few moments later, tossing his pencil aside.

"Okay, okay, I'll get there in a second."

Nels got up and walked to the window, leaning his arms on the sill. The road below was empty, waiting in the morning sunshine. Suddenly, wearily, he wished he didn't have a secret to keep—at least not such an important one, not such a troublesome one. One he couldn't share at *all*.

"There! That's done!" Alan said, propping his chart against a stack of books and pulling a scratch pad toward him. "Now, the next thing is to pick out a key word . . . What are you looking at? Somebody out there?"

"No," Nels said. He came back to look over Alan's shoulder. "What's a key word?"

"It can be any word you want, so long as it doesn't repeat a letter. N-E-L-S—we can use your name. That means we'll be using just four of the alphabets on the chart—the ones starting with those four letters, see? So now we write out the clear. Think up a message for me—a short one."

" 'Help, help, I am a prisoner in a sinister tower.' "

Alan half turned to give him a sardonic glance, then grinned and put down HAVING FAINTING FIT SEND HELP GLUP. Above that, as Nels started laughing in spite of himself, he wrote the key word over and over, matching each letter to one in the message, so that when Nels looked again, he saw:

```
n e l s n e l s n e l s n e l s n e l s n e l s n e l s n
H A V I N G F A I N T I N G F I T S E N D H E L P G L U P
```

"Okay," said Alan. "Now we start enciphering."

He began a fairly tedious process of locating a letter in the "clear" alphabet, then sliding a finger down to its equivalent in the appropriate "key" alphabet—it was a lot like locating addresses on a street map. Nels watched until he had caught onto the system, then idly watched Alan instead, studying the intent profile with its slightly snub nose and its wide, thin-lipped mouth—a mouth expressive as a cartoonist's pen line, which curled one way for scorn, another for mischief, turned up its corners in simple friendliness, tucked them deep with concentration, as now. A forelock of dark hair bobbed over one eye—that hair neither long nor short, brushing the collar of a shirt neither old-fashioned nor modern. He was a cryptogram himself, was Alan. But he's my friend, thought Nels with a sudden rush of affection. We may fight a little but I've never had a friend I felt this way about—as if I'd known him all my life.

Alan pushed his chart away. "Now. How's *that* for a cipher?" Nels took the paper, saw UEGAA KQSVR EAAKQ AGWPF QLPDC KWMCI, and said "Wow!"

"I thought you'd like the Vigenère," Alan said with satisfaction. "That 'I' on the end is just a null, I added it so the whole thing would divide evenly into five-letter segments—that's what real cryptographers do. Now, you can't tell me anybody is going to decode *that* in five minutes. Even your genius brother."

"Genius? I only said he was no dummy."

"Well—" Alan waved the subject aside.

"It's still going to make him curious, if he sees it lying around. This even *looks* like a cipher."

"So what if it does? Listen, do we have to give up the whole cipher thing, just because it might bug Stevie?" Alan sounded exasperated. He turned with an almost petulant movement and walked away to the window.

"Of course not," Nels said quickly. "I only meant . . . I didn't mean that." He started to go on, but hesitated, his eyes on Alan's sulky profile. But he's really my friend, he reminded himself. We just need to get this settled. Firmly, he went on, "The fact is, I've been sort of thinking about it, and I was wondering why we couldn't just—let Stevie in on it? I mean, he's actually a pretty good kid."

Alan turned in astonishment. "Let Stevie in on it? Let him come up here?"

"Well—why not? I mean actually? He—"

"It's impossible, that's why not." Alan gave a little laugh, shrugged helplessly. "Just plain impossible."

"Oh," Nels said.

There was a silence—Alan seemed to be waiting for the direct question Nels found he couldn't bring himself to ask. When the silence had made this clear to both of them, Alan leaned back against the worktable, half sitting on its edge, and smiled at Nels coaxingly. "Listen, Nels," he said. "What is all this about Stevie, anyhow? You know it wouldn't work out for him to come up here. The stuff we like to do is kind of too old for him, isn't it? He'd get bored. Then he'd want you to come on outdoors and do something different. And you wouldn't want to. And he'd go anyway. And you'd end up just the same—him outdoors and you up here—only he'd know the secret. What good would that do anybody?"

No good at all; Nels could see that plainly enough. "I guess you're right," he muttered.

"Sure I am. You've outgrown Stevie, that's what it is. Think how bored you get with checkers and bike riding and stuff he still likes. He's just got to realize it, that's all. He can't depend on you forever. It wouldn't even be good for him. He's got to learn to stand on his own feet, not hang on you all his life. You're not his entertainment committee. And he's not your responsibility, either."

"No," Nels agreed. "No, he's not. I've often thought that. I've often thought all those things."

"Well, sure you have," Alan said. "They're true, that's why. Stevie's just got to grow up a little. You're actually helping him, by coming up here—sort of forcing him to learn to be on his own."

"That's *so*," Nels said, much struck. The whole messy confusion of annoyance and guilt was suddenly swept from his mind, leaving the issue as clear as day, and himself blessedly detached. Alan's logic was a marvel. "I never realized that before."

"You would have, sooner or later. It's easier for me—I'm not involved."

"Yeah. Or just smarter," Nels added with a laugh. He was so relieved of worry he felt positively buoyant, as if he had only to kick off his shoes to float gently to the ceiling and bob about there. "Let's not waste any more time talking about it. How about I encipher something now?"

"Okay, what?"

"Oh, anything." Nels felt all amiability, as well as very close to Alan. It seemed impossible they had quarreled even for a minute. He sat down at the worktable, saw the pigtail strip of that morning's message, and reached for it. "I'll do this same one in the new cipher. 'Honorable escape expert invited to cookie party—' Hey, what happened to the cookie party?"

"It's coming," Alan promised. "Can't you smell? Mom's been baking all morning."

Nels raised his head and sniffed, then drew in a long and luxurious breath. How could he have failed to notice? The air was redolent of cookies. He could even distinguish the scents of cinnamon and anise, and a fresh, teasing whiff of some spice new to him. "They smell done," he said hungrily. "She'll be calling you to come for them any minute." Then all at once it was the right time to ask. "Why don't I ever see your mom?" he blurted. "Why doesn't she ever come in here? I'd like to meet her."

Alan said off-handedly, "She wants to meet you, too. That's the point of the cookie party. She'll be in pretty quick."

"She will?"

"Well, I hope so. I'm starving." He glanced past Nels toward the door and added, "Here she is. Come right on in!"

Nels whirled. A woman was coming carefully through the doorway, preceded by a loaded tray. He had one dazzled glimpse of rose-patterned cups, plates heaped with spangled, fancy cookies—then he raised his eyes to her face. He noticed nothing further. She was looking straight at him, smiling warmly, eagerly, with the hint of mischief that goes with springing a surprise. It was a wonderful smile—as if she had known him always, yet had only just found him. The strange thing was that he felt so too. Inside him it was as if some marvelous kind of flower were growing, expanding, opening huge quivering petals of color and light, and there was a burst of music and sunshine and relief, and people laughing.

Alan was laughing and his mother was saying, "Cookie party for honorable escape expert." Then she laughed too—the fluting ripple he had heard so often from the kitchen—and then they were all laughing, and Nels hurried over to help with the tray, feeling happier than ever in his life.

NELS WAS late for lunch—really late. Stevie had been sagging this way and that behind his chair for what seemed hours, listening to Rory and Jenny bicker and occasionally telling them crossly to shut up. Naturally they didn't do what *he* told them. It was getting so they didn't even do what Alice told them nowadays, unless she raised her voice at them, and she was beginning to make speeches about it pretty often. Eventually the uncle and aunt arrived, and asked the usual questions, and everybody sat down, and *still* Nels wasn't there.

"Stevie, do you know where your brother is?" Aunt Ruth demanded as if she suspected Stevie had taken Nels out and lost him. Stevie could only shrug and ask her defensively how *he* should know.

"Maybe he's in the bathroom," Jenny offered.

"Yeah, he's in the bathroom. He fell in!" Rory added crassly, which produced an eruption of giggles from him and Jenny, and a repressive, "Children!" from Aunt Ruth.

"Well, we'll just have to begin without him," Aunt Ruth said, and called Alice to serve the soup.

"Where does Nels *go*, anyhow?" Rory asked Stevie as they began to eat. "He's always gone somewhere."

"I wish I knew!" Stevie muttered.

"Let's follow him after lunch, and find out," Rory said with a sparkle beginning in his eye. "We'll never let him out of our sight, see? No matter what he says."

"He'll get mad," Stevie warned, but on second thought he decided he didn't care. "Okay, let's do."

"We'll really bug him!" Rory said. His dimple was coming and going, and his eyes were dancing as they always did when he was preparing to be a real pest, as he obviously was.

"I want to bug Nels too," Jenny said.

"No, you can't. This is only for Steve and me," Rory told her.

"Why is it? It is nah-aht," Jenny said belligerently, raising her voice.

"Children, please!" said Aunt Ruth. And at that moment Nels hurried in, looking a little flustered—but not flustered enough, Stevie reflected, without being quite sure what he meant. Aunt Ruth said, "*Well*, Nels!" and Nels muttered some sort of apology, sat down quickly, and picked up his soup spoon.

"Where were you?" Stevie asked, staring. Nels looked—well, excited, underneath his not-quite-flustered-enough expression. Excited and sort of happy, as if something good had happened.

"Oh, just—upstairs," Nels said in that vague tone that meant you were never going to get a bit more information.

"Whereabouts, upstairs?" Rory demanded. "I didn't see you. I was right in your room looking for Stevie, and it was only about one minute ago, and you weren't—"

"Forget it," Nels cut in. "Will you just forget it?"

"No I won't and you can't make me."

"Yeah, you're not our boss," Jenny chimed in.

"*Children*," said Aunt Ruth. After a reproving stare at each of them, she added in an excessively ladylike voice, "Now let's please just quiet down and eat our lunch."

Oh, gol, Stevie thought, mentally rolling his eyes up but not really doing it because it would only have made more waves, and anyhow he sort of saw Aunt Ruth's point. It got a person's stomach jumpy, having arguments at meals. Already he almost didn't want his soup. Nels, he noticed, wasn't really eating his, just stroking through it absently with his spoon, gazing at some spot in the air between himself and the salt cellar.

Stevie definitely didn't want his soup. He put his spoon down with a little clatter. At the same time, Uncle Fred put his down, slowly pushed back his bowl, eased his head against the chair back and smiled benevolently around the table. "Well children? Had a pleasant morning, did you?" Then the slight twinkle appearing under the overhanging eyebrows, the hint of a joke in the voice as he turned slowly, painfully toward Rory. "Hey, there, young man, what about it, can you spell 'receive'?"

"R-E-C-E-I-V-E," said Rory rapidly, without breaking his soup spoon's rhythmic rise and fall.

And just as predictably, Aunt Ruth said, "Fred, it's time for your yellow pill."

So lunch proceeded, with Nels in his trance and Rory and Jenny sniping at each other in undertones—Jenny looking cross and Rory fiendish, with dancing eyes. The minute they'd finished their ice cream and the four of them were allowed to leave the aunt and uncle to their coffee, Rory attached himself to Stevie with a reminding nudge and an air of carelessness so elaborate it would have warned even Ruffles that something was up. Nels wandered down the main hall to the game table and stopped irresolutely; Stevie and Rory kept at his heels and stopped there too. Rory at once launched into one of his monologues.

"Ah, ladies and gentlemen, we have started our famous Tour of the Inn," he announced rapidly under his breath, in what Stevie thought of as his TV-star manner—that is, with raised eyebrows and elegant gestures, dimples barely under control and eyes flicking sideways at Stevie to check the audience reaction. "A special tour for our famous visitor, Prince Nels the Dopey. At the moment we have stopped at the famous Game Table, where all the real famous game-players play famous games. I wonder why we have stopped? Per-hops to admire the view. Notice the beeyutiful view of the weeds out there, ladies and gentlemen. Or per-hops you would care for a game of checkers, my dear sir Prince? . . . No, I see we are not sticking around here, I wonder where we are going . . . oh, per-hops to the Rooftop Realty Company to buy us some realty. Are you interested in a little realty, my dear sir? No. Oh, well, never mind . . . I guess we have decided to go outdoors, but my dear sir, the roses are sort of cruddy at the moment, I do not think you will enjoy . . ."

And so on and so on, out the French doors and into the weedy rose garden, Nels wandering abstractedly in the lead, Rory gesturing and murmuring behind him, and Stevie trailing after, giggling helplessly and joining in when he could—though he wasn't much good at this kind of thing—and in his heart wishing hard that all of them were somewhere else doing something better. Jenny *was* somewhere else, having ostentatiously marched off down the main hall with her nose in the air, because by now she was crosser at Rory than she was at Nels. Those two were always getting cross at one another lately, Stevie thought. And then they got cross at everybody else too, and all because Nels never made them *quit*, the way he used to. He never did anything he used to. Right now, he wasn't even getting riled at Rory's needling, but just acted as if a fly was buzzing around, bothering him.

"What's the matter with you guys?" he asked remotely, after one of Rory's best quips. "Why don't you go play or something, and leave me alone?"

There was a tiny pause. "Oh, my dear sir," Rory began lightly. "My dear sir Prince—" but it came out flat and unfunny, as if somebody had let the air out—Stevie could see the whole game suddenly collapsing, watching Rory's face.

"Nothing's the matter with us," Stevie said. "We just wanted you to stick around and help us think of something to do. For once."

"I don't know what you mean, 'for once'," Nels said, still in that distant voice. "Listen, I'm not your entertainment committee. You're not my responsibility, either. You can't depend on me forever. It wouldn't even be good for you. You've got to learn to stand on your own feet, not hang on me all your life. I can't—"

"Okay, *okay*!" Stevie shouted. "Who's hanging on you? Who needs you anyway? I've got friends—guys a lot bigger and older than *you*. I'm going to meet them in just a little while. One of 'em might take me swimming in the river. Maybe even teach me to swim. In fact he might even—"

"The river? You're not supposed to go near the river, Aunt Ruth said so. None of us are."

"Well, I might go anyhow, so what do you think of that? No matter what dumb old Aunt Ruth or dumb old you, or—" Stevie might have gone on, wildly saying he knew not what, if

Jenny's voice had not sounded from the doorway, shrill and excited enough to capture even his attention.

"A package! A *package*!" she was crying. "Come on *in*, there's a package and it's for us!"

"I bet it's from Mommie!" Rory was already running. "Hey, Jen, is it from Mommie? Who's it from?"

Stevie started to follow, his mind abruptly full of his birthday, then full of his efforts not to think about his birthday because it was still three weeks away—then once more unhappily full of Nels. He halted and looked back. Nels was still standing beside the dirt-encrusted bird bath, looking nowhere in particular—as if it didn't even concern him.

"Aren't you coming?" Stevie demanded.

"Coming? Where?"

"Gol! To see what's in the *package* for us! *Gol*, Nels!"

"Oh. Sure." Nels came, not hurrying. But Stevie waited—made himself wait—until Nels was right beside him and they could go together through the French doors into the hall. The others were at the mail table—Aunt Ruth and Uncle Fred too.

"It's the gingerbread men!" yelled Rory, turning a face incandescent with joy. Jenny was joyfully yelling too, both of them tearing at the wrappings of the package and laughing so hard they nearly dropped it. In the end it was Stevie who took the lid off the box, and there they lay—three gingerbread men and one gingerbread lady, with icing hair and eyes and smiles and shoes, and beautiful red and gilt paper clothes—a special one for each child. Stevie realized he was grinning down at his man just as if it had been a person, an old friend—somebody he was as glad to see as he would have been to see Gram herself if she'd been alive, or even Mommie, almost.

"I *knew* she'd remember, I *told* you she would!" Jenny was repeating, over the hubbub made by Aunt Ruth exclaiming, and Uncle Fred rumbling questions, and Stevie answering them, and Rory singing a sort of grand opera solo in as near to a bass voice as he could get as he spun around and around with his gingerbread man just on the edge of Stevie's vision.

It broke off abruptly, song and movement together. Stevie looked around, startled, feeling everybody go still. It was a second before he realized that half of Rory's gingerbread man lay on the floor, shattered into crumbs. The top half was still in his hand, the gilt and red paper clothes hanging empty.

"Gol!" whispered Stevie, feeling shivery-glad it wasn't him it had happened to, but at the same time nearly dying for Rory. His fingers tensed around his own unharmed treasure, curled and cupped into an infinitely careful cradle.

"Oh, what a shame," Aunt Ruth said softly. Stevie could tell she really meant it. And Uncle Fred said something and kept patting Rory's shoulder. They all said something; Jenny edged up close beside Rory until their arms were touching, watching him with troubled eyes. He didn't move, just stood like wood, staring at the floor, with his head so far down you couldn't see anything but tousled fair hair and a glimpse of knotted, white-blond eyebrows, and the tips of his ears growing redder, and redder, and redder. Even when Aunt Ruth told him he could have one of the big Smiling Face suckers from the store, that cost a quarter, he didn't move or look up. He wasn't going to, either, Stevie knew. He might stay just like that for an hour, or all afternoon, and nothing anybody said would make him forget it or feel any better. It was the way he was. Stevie wished it was all over, wished and wished it had never happened. He saw a big tear splash on the floor between Rory's foot and the shattered gingerbread legs, and felt miserable, but there wasn't anything to do. He thought, I *hate* this day, it's an awful, hateful day.

Then Nels said, "Don't feel bad, Rory. Here, you can have mine." Almost carelessly, he said it. He walked over to

Rory and made him take the gingerbread man, saying, "Go on. I don't mind. Really. I don't care at all."

And he meant it. Stevie was staring right at him, as he walked away toward the stairs. You could tell he meant it. He didn't care at all. And somehow that was the worst thing that had happened yet.

V

AGMET

NELS WOKE, in the middle of the night a week or so later, to a nightmare sound. What he had heard he had no idea; he knew only that he was sitting bolt upright in bed, his breath held, his heart stopped—or so it felt—everything in him waiting for that noise to come again. It came. A loud, strange, strangled voice yelling "HELP!"

Nels struggled out of bed, gasping, tears bursting from his eyes, legs weak with fright. A woman's voice? His mother's voice it must be, though it was unrecognizable, so strange, so loud, so—emotionless. Where was she? Dad was hurting her this time, in all their fighting and screaming he had never hurt her before, but now he was, he was choking her . . .

"HELP!"

"Don't! Don't!" Nels sobbed. He was stumbling around in the chilly pitch-dark room trying to find the door. "Please! Stop! Don't!" He staggered against Stevie's bed, cried out and half fell onto it, clutching his knee, feeling Stevie squirm to life underneath him and heave around protestingly.

"HELP!"

"*Oh, no*!" Nels cried, and Stevie reared straight out of the covers, saying, "Gol! What is it?"

"It's them!" Nels said, on his feet, and groping toward the door again. "He's hurting her, they're fighting terrible, he'll kill her—"

"Who's 'them'?" Stevie said in a scared voice, scrambling after.

"Mommie and Dad, who else?"

"Mommie and Daddy—*here?*" Stevie's hand grabbed Nels's pajama top and clung tight.

"They must be! We've got to find her. Let *go!*" Nels screamed—he felt he was screaming, but he wasn't making much noise, only a breathy queer bleat—another nightmare sound.

"HELP!"

Just that one word, he thought wildly, why just the one word, why doesn't she say something else ever, why doesn't it change some way . . .

Stevie let go. "But it can't be them. That's outside!" His voice suddenly came from over by the window. "It's something outdoors."

"No, it's not, they wouldn't be outdoors . . ."

"But it's not them! They aren't here, wake up! This is something else."

At once, a part of Nels that *had* still been asleep—his brain, perhaps—woke up, told him that this was Reeves Ferry, that his mother was miles away, his father too, both of them safe and sane. Even the darkness of the room swung around and settled into its usual pattern, with the dresser dimly perceived there, and the door there. But his heart had begun a thick pounding, and he was shaking all over. When the raucous "HELP!" pierced the night again, he felt his way to his bed on trembling legs and sank down on the edge. It was still a nightmare sound.

"Is it some kids out in the road?" Stevie was saying. He pushed the window up another half-inch—it was warped, and would never go more than halfway—and tried to thrust his head out. "I wish it would last a little longer, so we could tell what . . ." He pulled his head back abruptly. "Hey, the others are up. Listen."

Nels, too, had caught the sound of voices—Rory's high one over a mixture of Aunt Ruth's and Uncle Fred's. Stevie was across the room in an instant, the door flung wide. Nels followed him quickly. In a pool of dim light at the head of the main stair, the others were clustered—Aunt Ruth, unfamiliar in bathrobe and pink hairnet, Uncle Fred with his ordinary daytime cane in odd contrast to rumpled pajamas, Rory and Jenny shivering and barefoot, and huddling close to each other and Aunt Ruth.

"Hey, did you hear it?" Stevie cried as he ran to join them. "What was it? What's out there?"

Rory and Jenny turned eyes like saucers. "A bird, she says! Wow, wasn't it spooky? Wow, Jenny and me were scared! I didn't know what it *was*. I—"

They had a lot more to say, but Stevie cut through it. "A *bird?* Gol, how could that be a *bird*?"

"A peacock, dear." Aunt Ruth explained. "We think—Rory, *hush*, I can't hear myself think—we believe it must be one of the Johnsons' peacocks, got loose from its pen or wherever they keep them. It *is* an awful noise, I trust it won't go on all—Fred, I do wish you'd go back to bed, you'll catch a chill! I should get your slippers—"

"There it is again!" Rory cried, half drowning out the sound and preventing anybody from telling where it came from.

"The back, I think! Must be out in those trees," Stevie exclaimed, and nearly knocked Nels down dashing for the tall windows across the hall from their room.

"No, no, I think it's out front," came Uncle Fred's rumble.

"Maybe in the big fir?" Rory hazarded. He dashed after Steve, Jenny at his heels. "Hey, Stevie, it's in the big fir, maybe, the one by the dining room. Uncle Fred says. Let's go downstairs, come on! Aunt Ruth, can we go downstairs? Can we go outside and catch it? Only will you come too? Hey, Jen—"

Nels tuned him out, tuned out all the high, excited babbling, and Aunt Ruth's distracted answers, and her anxious clucking over Uncle Fred, who was ignoring her and starting for the stairs, drawing them all along in a little swirling clump, like electrons around a nucleus. Nels leaned against the linen closet door and closed his eyes, feeling dazed and sore, almost sick, as if something terrible had been going on for hours and hours. As if somebody had died, or there'd been a car accident, or he'd been crying for a long time. Peacock. It couldn't be a peacock, that didn't make sense. Peacocks lived in zoos. Or fairy tale books. Not Reeves Ferry, in the middle of the night . . . Nothing made sense, and he didn't want to struggle with it. He crept back along the hall to his room, hesitated as he heard the excited voices through the open window, finally went over to kneel beside it. They were all outside now, beside the big fir tree, staring up and pointing; the floodlight was on. Looking straight across from his vantage point Nels could see, after a moment or two of searching, a patch of thicker dark among the fir's dark branches, about halfway up. And then the shapes sorted themselves out and quite suddenly he saw it—a slim, large bird, astonishingly large, with tapering neck and long downward sweep of folded tail—just sitting there in the tree.

"HELP!" came the piercing cry again—just as awful as ever, just as weirdly emotionless, just as desperate, just as nightmarish. Nels went cold and shivery, totally unable to connect the sound with the big, graceful shape and make it a bird calling. The shape was a mere incongruity, the sound was a murdered soul wailing. There was a burst of exclamations from under the tree, and Stevie's excited laugh, and his voice saying, "Gol, it's creepy, isn't it? Nels thought it was—" The voice broke off abruptly, came back defiant: "Nels thought it was some dumb fight or something, somebody getting killed!" Rory and Jenny responded with some rather scared laughter. And Nels tuned them all out again.

He was still there, kneeling by the window with his head on his folded arms, when Stevie came back however long a time later it was, asking why he hadn't come down, and talking about the peacock still in the fir tree, and Uncle Fred saying he'd telephone the Johnsons in the morning. He had a lot to say but Nels kept it all at a distance, just got in his bed and shut his eyes. But he couldn't sleep, not even after Stevie had quieted down and begun to breathe slow and even. He kept hearing that chilling cry again, as if for the first time, and living over and over his fright, his helpless stumbling around, his irrational conviction that it was his father killing his mother. It got worse instead of better. Outside, the peacock screamed again, and he was out of bed, knowing he couldn't stand to stay here listening.

Then he remembered that Alan had asked him to come at night sometime, to try the telescope.

It was so easy, so obvious, that even as he was running silently along the dark hall he marveled that he hadn't done it before. Night was a perfect time, really; nobody around to sneak away from, nobody to wonder where he'd gone. In a minute he had slipped behind the carved screen and down the passage into the General's room, and Alan turned from the front window, a pale smudge of face and hands in the shadows.

"Good! I thought you might come. Did you hear that crazy commotion?"

"Yeah, a peacock!" Nels smothered a laugh—it was suddenly just funny, cockeyed, no more alarming than a cow mooing or a rooster crowing unexpectedly. "It belongs to the Johnsons. Who are they, anyhow?"

"Oh, they live up river. It must have got away, I suppose. Wonder why they want to raise the things?"

"I can't imagine!" Nels said with feeling. "Can we look through the telescope?"

"Sure! Come on, my dad's already got it set up. He's studying Saturn."

His dad, Nels thought as they went through the bookcase door. I'm going to see his dad! And *this* time I'll look at this room as we go through . . .

But this time it was night. The room behind the bookcase, which had never been more than a blur of light and color to him, was now dark like everyplace else. Only the window, a tall rectangle powdered with stars, guided them to the corner where the stairs spiraled up. Never mind, Nels told himself. I'll look when I come down. At least I remembered!

Little by little, he was remembering to notice everything; the outlines of Alan's world were gradually filling in, right out to the edges. But it was a world so ambiguously like and unlike his own that the key clue he had hoped for seemed farther away than ever. He was beginning to wonder if it mattered. Suppose the riddle stayed unsolved? Who cared?

Tonight, when they reached the dark little hexagonal hall, Alan opened the door to the living room, instead of his own. The room was full of starlight, shining through its three tall windows; in the middle one, Nels saw the long, thin silhouette of a small telescope angling up and outward from spidery legs. A pale blur detached itself from the shadows and became Alan's mother, in her nightclothes like the rest of them, with her cropped dark hair rumpled, her eager smile the same.

"Come on in! It's a perfect night for it, and Alan's dad has focused right on Saturn and it's fantastic! Those rings are so plain . . . Honey? Honey, here's Nels, Alan's friend, let him have a look!"

Gently she drew Nels toward the window, and a lanky figure in a bathrobe turned to greet him. Nels had an impression of a rugged, cordial face, a vast hand enveloping his, a warm deep voice saying, "Well, hello, Nels! Heard a lot about you.

Alan says he couldn't have finished that plane without you."

"Oh—" Nels shrugged deprecatingly, though he could feel his cheeks heating with pleasure. "I didn't really do much. He had it almost finished before I ever saw it."

"You had the idea about using plastic for the bubble," Alan put in.

"But *you* thought of the cleaning bags."

Alan's father laughed. "You're both great idea-men. Tell you what—you'll have to build a moon rocket next. Or an interplanetary spaceship, how's that for a project? Take you right to Mars. Or Saturn. Ever had a peek at Saturn before, Nels?"

"No, never. I've never even looked through a really good telescope before."

"Well, here's your chance. Just put your eye right there, and if it's blurry, twiddle with that little knob . . ."

And then he was looking into the whirling mysteries of space, and everything and everybody else receded into unimportance.

Later, when the four of them sat around the kitchen table eating cinnamon toast and watching the first streaks of dawn replace the stars in the window, Nels said out of a full heart, "Oh, I wish it could always be right now! I don't want anything to be different, ever, I don't want it to get to be today, then tonight, then tomorrow—"

Alan burst out laughing. "That'd leave you eating this one breakfast forever."

"Okay, fine, I'd be glad to," Nels said recklessly. "So long as it never gets daylight and nobody leaves the table—"

They were all laughing at him by now. Alan said, "You nut, what about our cipher we're inventing? We've got to work on that later on, when you come back up."

"Yes, you can come *right* back up again," Alan's mother

reminded him. "As soon as you've had your—downstairs breakfast."

"I know, but . . ." Nels couldn't quite say what he meant. He looked around the blue-and-white checked kitchen—new to him this morning, yet he seemed to have known it always—and at the rose-patterned dishes and the three friendly faces turned to him. Three new-old friends they were, linked to him and to each other in affection and warmth and humor and the shared experiences of the night, the stars, the wonder of Saturn, the lovely homely bliss of cinnamon toast. "It's just . . . I hate to think of leaving. You know, going back to the city. School starting. All that."

There was a startled little silence, Then Alan exclaimed, "But you're not leaving very soon?"

"Well—not till the end of the month."

They all looked at him in concern, Alan in dismay. "The end of August? And here it is the eleventh already! No, the twelfth!"

"That gives us three more weeks or so."

"It's not enough! Oh, who wants to go to some old *city*?"

"Alan!" said his mother gently. "Nels may prefer the city."

"No, I *don't*," Nels told her. "But . . ."

"But that's where you'll be going anyhow," she finished for him. "Well, it's a shame."

He was wishing he hadn't brought it up—reminded himself of it. "I don't exactly know where I'll be going," he said uncomfortably. "But I know I'll be leaving here—can't stay around forever."

"I don't see why not," Alan said. Suddenly he burst out, "Nels, don't go!"

"No, don't!" his mother agreed impulsively. "Live here with us. Be Alan's brother. We've always wanted two boys, haven't we, honey?"

"Sure we have!" Alan's father said.

"Oh, *great*!" Alan shouted. "I'll let you sleep on the bottom bunk, okay? And I've got plenty of spare clothes—can you wear my shoes, d'you think? Or maybe we could—"

"I'm sure we can manage some private, exclusive shoes for Nels, when the need arises," his father put in solemnly, and the other two started laughing.

Nels hesitated, and then laughed too. Of course they were only joking, tossing a lovely impossible fantasy from one to the other just for the fun of it. They knew as well as he that it could never happen. But it was nice—it was more than nice—to know they truly wished it could. Stumbling a bit, he tried to tell them so. "I mean, I know you aren't really serious, but—"

"Of course we're serious," Alan's mother said, and then nobody was laughing, and Nels could see they actually meant it, they were inviting him to live with them.

"But—how could I?" he asked, bewildered.

"Simple," Alan retorted. "Just don't go back downstairs."

Nels stared at him, suddenly breathless with an alarm as powerful as it was unreasoned. "Oh, I *couldn't*," he gasped. "I—Stevie—"

"Oh, *Stevie*. Forget Stevie for once! Listen—no, wait Nels, let me tell you—"

Firmly, his father's voice cut in. "Alan, don't press him. He's not ready yet. Let him think about it."

"But Dad!"

"Your father's right," Alan's mother agreed. She smiled at Nels, and his alarm subsided; he could feel the little hairs on the back of his neck begin to settle down. "He knows we want him. That's enough for now. You just take your time, Nels. Meanwhile, have some more cinnamon toast."

"Okay—thanks," Nels murmured, smiling back at her. Slowly his comfort was restored. It was still only breakfast time of this best of all visits, and there was a whole three weeks to go. With a glance at the pearl-streaked, dark rose sky, he bit a huge crunchy corner off his fresh triangle of toast and began to talk to Alan about their cipher.

Before full daylight he was slipping back along the silent hall, into the dimness of his own room, into his chilly bed. Stevie's breathing, and an occasional snuffle, came undisturbed from the tangle of covers which was all Nels could see of him. Nobody was awake yet. Nobody had even known he was gone. Gradually his own bed warmed, and a delicious drowsiness crept over him, and his eyelids closed.

When he awoke Stevie was already dressed and outdoors, under the big tree with Rory and Jenny. Nels could hear their voices, still talking about the peacock; evidently somebody was on the way over to collect it. When he looked out, he could see the big bird, on a lower branch now. It was moving about a little, grooming itself, turning its jewel-like head in tiny, indignant jerks, appearing restless. Even as he watched, it lifted astonishingly wide wings, flapped noisily out of the tree, raising a chorus of excited chatter below, and sailed straight across to the roof of the store—the flat strip just under the windows of the west wing passage. It made a clumsy landing on the bar of the pointy iron railing.

"HELP!" it yelled, then just stood there looking beautiful and stupid in the early sun.

Nels drew back from the window, feeling merely bored with it now, and hurried into his clothes. He hoped whoever was coming showed up right away. He wanted to get back to the tower and the new cipher the minute breakfast was over, and all this other was a waste of time.

Mr. Johnson and his son came, just as everybody was leaving the breakfast table. They had pans of grain and lots to say about peacocks and definite plans for catching this one from inside, through the west passage windows. Everybody trooped upstairs to watch the performance; There was not a chance of getting away. Stifling his impatience, Nels hung around with the others, and eventually the big bird was brought outlandishly right through the window into the house, and carried along the passage in Mr. Johnson's arms with its improbable tail almost trailing the threadbare carpet. Finally, after a pause for admiration and cautious touching, it was borne down the front stairs and out, with everybody tagging along to keep it in sight until the very last minute.

Everybody except Stevie. Exasperatingly, he stayed there on the top step beside Nels, and when Nels edged away down the hall, he found Stevie moving along with him, talking, talking, still excited about the peacock, wishing it hadn't been caught so soon, wishing *he* had a pet of some kind here, even a peacock—even a *chicken*—saying something about the mantis he and Nels had kept that time, and about a box or cage or something he was working on . . . And at last, at last, he left Nels standing by the rear hall windows and darted into their room to fetch whatever it was to show him.

Nels didn't wait, even long enough for ordinary caution. As if released from a spring he fled down the creaking hall and behind the screen to the General's room. Alan was at the window, watching the Johnsons' pickup recede up Ferry Road. As he turned, Nels said hurriedly, "Let's go—Stevie's practically right behind me, I couldn't—"

He broke off. Footsteps were pounding along the hall, a joyful voice calling triumphantly, "I know where you are! I saw you go in there!"

"Inside, quick!" whispered Alan, leaping for the bookcase.

Nels was treading on his heels, crowding in beside him, tugging the bookcase till it touched its latch. It had barely stopped moving when Stevie's voice sounded just on the other side of it—right in the General's room.

"Nels?" Then, less confidently, "Hey, Nels."

Huddled breathless in the musty dark behind the bookcase, Nels felt Alan quiver with sudden mirth, struggled to suppress his own. They'd made it, but only *just* . . . What a narrow squeak! Cautiously he eased his cramped position, felt Alan grip his shoulder, heard a barely audible "shhh." Clamping a hand over his mouth to hold back the laughter, he waited, every muscle tense. Beyond, in the room, uncertain footsteps—over toward the window, back to the middle of the room, a sudden little rush: "*I* know where you are, you're under the bed, so come on out, I—" A pause, an even more uncertain "Nels? Hey, I give up. Come *on*."

There followed a long silence. Then one broken word—"*Gol*," that was at once bitter, bewildered, despairing. Nels's inward mirth faded. He wanted only to leave, now, go quickly to the tower. But before he could move, another sound checked him—a soft, rising wail of hurt and disappointment so intense, so painful and private that it suddenly became his own pain, sweeping through him unendurably. He straightened, groped for the coat hook so he could go out, go to Stevie.

Beside him, Alan snickered.

Nels whirled fiercely in the darkness. "Don't laugh at him! Shut up!"

"Shut up yourself, dummy!" came the answering hiss. "D'you want him to hear?"

"I don't care, I—"

"Come *on*. Quick!"

The hand clamped his shoulder hard enough to hurt, pulled him, shoved him toward the crack of light widening in the back of the closet—and then they were in that other room, running together toward the spiral stairs and up them, Alan like a watchdog at his heels.

Once in Alan's room, they faced each other, breathless.

"Why did you do that?" Nels's voice was shaking. "I'm going back down! You shouldn't laugh at him!"

"You can't go right now—you'll run straight and tell him everything, and be sorry later. He'll get over it! He's probably already—"

"You don't know Stevie! You don't know anything about him, *anything*."

"Oh, all right, I don't, but why d'you want to wreck our fun? Nels, *please* don't do it. Don't go. You'll feel different pretty soon. Remember this morning."

Nels hesitated, remembering this morning—the whirling stars, the wonderful breakfast, the firm, warm feeling of affection that had lapped him like a blanket. "I didn't say I'd—tell him anything. Just go *be* with him awhile. I could come back later."

"No. You couldn't. Not today, not any time all day long. I—wouldn't be here."

Nels stared at him. "Wouldn't be here?"

"Listen, I can't explain, you'll just have to believe me. If you leave now, it'll be—I don't really know how long, maybe longer than a day, maybe two days, maybe even more. And there's something I want *like anything* to do—I mean for both of us to do, and my dad's only going to be around *today*—"

"Your dad? What does he have to do with it?"

"He's going to help us. He promised he would. You want to guess what it is?"

Alan was beginning to smile eagerly, a sparkle of excitement in his eyes. And going back downstairs was beginning to seem a little less important. At least, going back right now. I could leave early instead, Nels thought. That might even be better. I'll go down in time to play checkers or something with Stevie before lunch, and I'll *stay* down all afternoon. Do whatever he wants. He's probably gone by now anyhow . . . Automatically, he glanced out the window toward the road. And there was the foreshortened figure on the bike, not dawdling this time but pedaling furiously, the bright head bent over the handlebars, elbows high and tense, legs pumping.

"You see?" Alan said. "I told you he'd get over it."

But he wasn't over it—Nels knew the signs. The face that could not be seen from up here would be bright red, the blue eyes still swimming. He was working it off, that was all. "You didn't have to laugh at him," Nels muttered resentfully.

"Well, I'm sorry. It was—it just struck me funny, I don't know why. I won't, ever again. Honest."

He sounded contrite, and looked so, too, when Nels met his eyes. Anyway, Stevie was out of reach—halfway to the schoolgrounds by this time—what was done was done. But I'll leave good and early, Nels resolved. "Okay," he said to Alan. "It was all my fault anyhow—I wasn't careful enough getting away. So what's this thing your dad's going to help us with?"

"Can't you guess? Remember, last night when we were talking about the plastic bubble for the plane, and Dad said we were great idea-men, and we'd have to build a moon rocket next, or—" Alan waited with an expectant grin.

"Or an interplanetary spaceship!" Nels quoted, staring. "Your dad's going to help us build a *spaceship*?"

"Well, only a mock-up of course. Like old Ruby the Spitfire. D'you want to?"

"Do I *want* to?" Nels felt as though he were vibrating all over with the strength of his wanting to. "What—what's it going to look like? There's two or three ways we could—"

"We have to design it. Right now! Because he'll be here by noon to help us start it. See? That's why I—"

"Yes, I see," Nels said hastily. "Well—listen, I used to draw a kind of spaceship that might be okay. I've worked on it a lot. Here, I'll show you . . ." He dropped into his chair at the worktable, rummaged in the drawer for pencil and paper, and began to draw the design he'd worked on all last year at home, never dreaming he'd ever see it anywhere but on paper. "What are we going to build it of?" he asked as he worked.

"Oh, scrap lumber and chicken wire, I suppose—same as Ruby." Alan was hanging over his shoulder. "Wow. It's round? Conical, I mean?"

"They always are. They wouldn't go, otherwise, there'd be friction. What's wrong with being conical?"

"Kind of hard to build, maybe."

"The Spitfire's nose is conical."

"That's so. Sure, we can do that. Hey, I want to design one too, then we can pick the best—or maybe sort of combine them." Alan flung himself into the other chair, began eagerly on his own ship.

Glancing at it occasionally as it progressed, Nels saw that it, too, was basically conical—in fact, cigar-shaped. He'd experimented with cigar forms, but they seemed to him inefficient. His own ship was a compact, sturdier shape, much like that of the ink bottle on the worktable, which swelled to its broadest circumference a third of the way up from its base, then tapered sharply to its sliced-off top. There, closely resembling the ink bottle's cap, was the huge fan to power the air engine. Nels was trying to draw its overlapping blades when Alan demanded to know what that thing was.

"Fan. For when you're inside the atmosphere. It collects air in this chamber, see, and shoots it down the pipe, clear through the middle of the ship to this air engine on the bottom."

"But what's it for?"

"Conserves fuel—as long as you're in the atmosphere—and then you get this hover action when you're landing."

"Neat," Alan murmured. He studied Nels's drawing thoughtfully, then went back to his own and erased something. After a moment he scrapped his whole drawing, beginning fresh on another sheet of paper.

Nels smiled to himself. Alan's second design would probably be much closer to his own. Well, it seemed only right that he should take the lead, for once. He felt himself more knowledgeable than Alan in the field of space technology, if in no other. And speaking of space technology, Nels reflected, staring critically at his own drawing, I've forgotten to leave a space for my computers. He did a little erasing himself, then checked everything over: computers, control room, weapons room, dining room, living quarters, space for at least five gyroscopes and six big fuel tanks . . . and I wonder about the fuel, Nels pondered. Something that will conduct electricity, so it'll be expended slowly—an acid, it would have to be. Maybe hydrochloric? Sulphuric? . . . I wish I knew more about acids.

It was Alan, not he, who heard the lunch bell two hours later. And by the time he'd made a last hurried revision on his design, Alan's father had come, and had to be shown the two plans, and arrangements had to be made for Nels to return the instant the meal was over, to discuss the actual construction. Far from leaving earlier than usual, he was late again for lunch.

The sight of Stevie, slumped there in his chair dabbling without interest at his soup, came as a blow that knocked him breathless. He stood shocked and bewildered, like a bird that has thudded into a window pane, until Aunt Ruth's voice prodded him to his seat, then he kept thinking stupidly, *I forgot. I forgot all about him. I was going to come down early—play checkers or something. Because I felt bad about—what happened.* Only he found he could not quite remember what had happened—not clearly, because that would make him feel worse, much worse, and what was the use of that, unless Stevie brought it up or something . . .

Stevie made no mention of it—or of anything else. He ate his way indifferently through his lunch, answered Uncle Fred's ritual question, passed things when he was asked, and neither spoke to Nels nor looked at him. But he didn't seem angry, just . . . just very . . . Nels shied away from trying to pin down what Stevie seemed instead of angry, because something about it hurt him worst of all, and it was a panicky kind of pain. I won't think about it, Nels told himself quickly. It's all past now. I mustn't think of it again.

THAT SAME afternoon Alan's father, after a study of their two designs, drew up some construction plans and got them started on the new project. Next morning he produced a supply of scrap lumber and chicken wire, promised to rig a pulley system when the time came, and left them to it.

For Nels, the best part of the summer then began, as the days passed, bright beads on a string, filled with happy, absorbing work. Only one thing marred his peace of mind—that was the strange, painful little jolt he got now, every time he saw Stevie. Every lunchtime, every afternoon when he reluctantly came downstairs for dinner and the evening, he was brought up short by another bruising thud into that windowpane. Like repeatedly bumping a sore toe, it grew more painful instead of less.

But on the other hand the hurt never lasted long, and once it eased, he was all right until the next time.

It was essentially Nels's design that was gradually taking shape in the middle of Alan's room, though the working plans combined elements from both drawings. As Nels had expected, Alan's second one was very similar to his own, but included a number of refinements Nels had rejected as nonessential—for instance, a small rocket attached perpendicularly below the main engine, to propel the ship sideways if necessary, and a special small fuel tank for powering the food-making machines. Nels reconsidered these two and agreed to them, but not to the more fanciful ones that Alan kept trying to introduce later, high-handedly discarding necessities to do so.

"How come we need all this space for gyroscopes?" he asked Nels impatiently one day when he was trying to find room for mini-craft. "A gyroscope isn't very big, is it? What do they look like?"

Nels could only stare for a second; Alan was remarkably ignorant in spots. Describing a gyroscope seemed impossible. Flipping through the General's old book on military aircraft, which they often consulted, he silently pointed to a diagram.

"Oh!" Alan said in a baffled voice. "Wheels within wheels!" —which was a fair description after all. "Well, do we have to have *five* of them? What do they do?"

"They keep the ship level, for one thing. And once they're started, they have a sort of pulsing action—it generates electricity. Enough to keep them going awhile, and run other things on the ship too."

"Like for instance?" Alan persisted.

"Like for instance the *engines*."

"Oh." Alan grinned, and abandoned that tack. "Okay, we need lots of space for gyroscopes." His eyes were already running over the master plan again. "But does a computer take all this room? Do we *need* a computer?"

Nels took a grip on his patience. "We need one if we want to plan how many orbits we ought to make on a certain trip, and what shape they should be, and . . . . Besides, how else are we going to know if anything goes wrong?"

"The computer can tell that?"

"Well, sure! Look. It's programmed to take electric charges for *everything* on the ship. So if something goes wrong, right away it eliminates all the correct numbers of charges—all the okay ones, see?—and finds the incorrect one. Then it flashes a red light—and you know Number Four engine is malfunctioning."

Alan looked reluctantly impressed, and agreed that they needed a computer. "*You* find some place to carry the mini-craft, then, if you know so much," he added with a tinge of irritation that Nels found suddenly disarming. It *was* irritating when somebody always knew all the answers. Why was he resisting Alan's mini-craft anyway? They were partners in this—and he was clearly captain, so he ought to be generous.

"We could steal some space from one of the fuel tanks," he conceded. "I think we can put a launching door right here."

So once more their heads were bent together over the drawings, and their differences forgotten—until the next time Alan wanted to scrap something Nels knew to be essential. Nels sometimes wondered if Alan knew any more about spaceships than Rory. Maybe, like Rory, he didn't really want to know all that much. He might secretly prefer ciphers, or old Ruby, or stars. And one afternoon it occurred to Nels that the old pocket-of-time theory might explain it. Fifty years ago, such things as computers and lasers hadn't been invented. Therefore, Nels plodded on in his reasoning, there was a strong likelihood . . .

And right then Nels discovered that at some point during these busy days—or weeks?—of building, he had lost all interest in clues and theories and the riddle of Alan. He wanted only to accept. Alan was undeniably *here*, beside him in this tower room. And the glorious interplanetary spaceship he had doodled and dreamed of on paper was here, too, taking actual, solid form before his eyes on the shabby carpet—and Alan's ignorance, whatever the cause, was keeping *him* captain. How could anybody wish for more?

Lovingly—but critically—he studied the skeletal framework. It was almost complete by now; Alan was fastening the last lengths of chicken wire. "Tomorrow we'll be starting on the outside," Nels remarked. He was visualizing the inside, too—the astronauts, even passengers, in the circular control room, and their needs. "We'll have to find some means of keeping the air in. We could use metal, maybe. A metal skin . . . And something to keep the radiation *out*. We'd better seal the wood first, then put on the metal skin. That ought to do it."

"Where are we going to get this metal skin?" Alan demanded, stepping back to survey their work. "I know! That metalic paint we used on Ruby!"

"Foil would be better. Would your mother have any kitchen foil? Just that plain old—" He broke off as Alan shook his head. "Okay, okay, then I'll bring some from the store. I've got my allowance."

"Won't everybody want to know why you want it?"

"No, they . . ." But Nels could almost hear Aunt Ruth: *Freezer foil? Now what on earth can the child want with freezer foil?* "I'll make some excuse," he said, and added, "We haven't even thought of a name for the ship."

"I have. What about 'The Martian Eye'?" Alan turned with a grin. "And I was thinking—we could paint the name on the ship in cipher, that cipher we made up ourselves—just to make it more secret, you know."

"Oh, great! And right beside it, paint a real weird red eye."

"Encipher it right now, so we can see what it looks like. I'll finish this." Alan returned to his chicken wire, and Nels hurried to the worktable to find the cipher charts they had worked out. He flicked a routine glance out the window—and there was Stevie, pedaling in aimless circles on the road below. Nels recoiled, feeling everything in him draw in tight from the now-familiar pain. It was almost a physical pain, and some other, deeper kind besides, and it *kept* coming back and back—as if the bird could not learn that there was glass in that window instead of empty sunshine, and was gradually battering itself to death. There seemed no way to guard against it—short of going about blindfold, so as not to see Stevie. But he had to find some way; he had to get over it, he told himself angrily. It was stupid—and it was the only thing left that disturbed him since the ship-building started. Just this thing about neglecting Stevie.

Why can't I just quit worrying about it? Nels thought. It isn't even my fault!

He spread out the cipher charts—feeling, in spite of himself, a stirring of resentment against Alan, whose fault it *was*. Why was it so impossible to let Stevie in on it? Nobody else at all, just Stevie. Then nothing would hurt me any more, thought Nels. I wouldn't have to worry about a thing.

Gradually, as his pencil found the proper letters in the chart, and his mind fastened onto its job, the sore ache faded, and the tight-drawn part of him began to ease. By the time he had transposed "The Martian Eye" into AGM ETPVRTF CXC and divided it into the professionally proper five-letter units filled out with his own and Alan's initials as nulls, he had forgotten Stevie.

"Have a look at this!" he exclaimed, turning triumphantly with his finished cipher, which now read AGMET PVRTF CXCNA.

Alan looked, and gave a shout of laughter. "We can call it Agmet for short. Let's christen it when it's finished. With lemonade." With a jerk of his head toward the ship, he added, "It won't be long. Day after tomorrow we'll be ready for the foil."

Nels gazed at the skeletal "Agmet" and drew a deep breath of satisfaction. "I'll get hold of some. Best thing would be to go in the store early, soon as it's open—Aunt Ruth's always too busy then to pay much attention. Okay—day after tomorrow. It might make me a little late, but I'll have it when I come up."

AUNT RUTH," Stevie said next morning. "Can I have this kind today, instead of that one?"

"Kind of what? Oh, cookies. Let me see what you've got." Hand still busy twisting fasteners around plastic bags of dried prunes, Aunt Ruth frowned absently at the box of vanilla wafers Stevie was holding up. "Thought you liked the Fig Newtons best. They're better *for* you."

"But there's more in this box," Stevie explained.

"My conscience! What do you need with any more? Question is, how you manage to get away with the number you do eat, between breakfast and lunchtime—every day of this world—"

"These are only a nickel more. I've got a dime upstairs," Stevie added on a sudden thought. "I'll go—"

"No, no, child, for heaven's sakes, I don't want your dime. I just wonder if you ought to snack so much, is all."

"Oh, let it go, Ruth. He's a growing boy," Uncle Fred leaned slowly, slowly to one side until he could see around the cash register to wink and nod at Stevie. "Feller's got to keep his strength up, isn't that right, young man?"

Stevie smiled back and muttered, "Yeah," feeling rather guilty. Then as Aunt Ruth gave her customary, "Well, all right, now run along and don't fiddle with things," he divided a thank you scrupulously between them, and went on outdoors.

On his way around to the service yard to get his bike, he looked again at the box of wafers, shook it dubiously. It *said* there were twelve ounces inside—he didn't know how many cookies that meant, but more than in the Fig Newton package, anyway. Certainly enough to go around without breaking any in two. Wally hadn't liked that yesterday—having only a half-cookie. And Sam, the tall yellow-haired sunburned one who made most of the funny remarks, had made several—not really very funny—about Stevie putting them on a diet.

Gol, why can't he bring some, then? Stevie thought indignantly. There were four extra people yesterday.

There were always a few boys there at the playground, but their numbers shifted unpredictably. It was really just a meeting place, and a bike-fixing workshop. How it had also got to be a handout place for refreshments—with him always treating—Stevie didn't know.

Well, he did know. It was because he'd happened to be eating a Fig Newton as he rode into the playground one morning—a couple of weeks ago, way before the peacock night—and Wally or somebody had asked him what he had there, so of course he'd passed around what was left. The next time he'd brought some

Fig Newtons on purpose, as a sort of offering. It had seemed logical enough, even fair, like buying your ticket to get in. And they'd let him stay, without much objection—some of them even thanked him for the cookies—so he'd just kept on bringing some every day. Now they'd got to expecting it, and if he didn't bring enough they bugged him about it. And that *wasn't* fair. It was—something else, something that made Stevie feel sort of rebellious and shamefaced both at the same time, and gave him half a notion to show up without anything once, and let them like it or lump it.

On the other hand . . . He dropped the vanilla wafers into his basket and wheeled the bike out of the service yard, hopping on one foot till he had a start and then flinging his leg over. He knew it wasn't just because of the cookies they let him come. He could tell. They sort of liked him, some of them. That Bob, the one who never said anything, but who knew the most about motors—he let Stevie hold things sometimes, wrenches and screws, and let him stand right there close and watch him fix things. It was probably because of finding out Stevie's dad flew airplanes.

That came up one morning when a plane buzzed the Inn on its way south, dipping low enough for Stevie to see the familiar gray and blue stripes. Without thinking, he exclaimed. "Hey, there's my dad!"

"Your dad!" Wally echoed. He squinted upwards. "That's a Ames-Anderson Freightways plane. He work for them?"

"Yeah. It's his company," Stevie explained. Then remembering, he added, "Used to be."

Several of the boys had turned to listen. Lloyd, the big one, said, "No joke? Your dad is Ames?"

"Anderson. Mr. Ames is his partner. Used to be," Stevie added doggedly.

"What's this 'used to be'?" Wally put in, laughing a little. "You mean it's *not* his company any more?"

"Not exactly." Stevie didn't know how to answer. There was something called Hands of the Receivers. And his dad had said he worked for the bank now, but kind of laughed when he said it. "Maybe it's the bank's," Stevie hazarded.

There was a puzzled little silence. Then Ernie said, "You mean he went broke?"

"Yeah, I guess so," Stevie said.

There was another pause. Somebody said, "That's tough, kid," and several voices muttered, "Yeah."

"It doesn't matter, he's going to pay it all back," Stevie told them. "Then it'll be his again. He still flies his same routes and all anyhow."

"He ever take you up with him?" Lloyd asked suddenly.

"Sure. He's taken all of us. Nels most, though—my brother Nels. He used to let Nels fly sometimes. You know, sort of steer."

"Hey, neat!" Lloyd said. "Wow, I wish my dad could fly a plane. All he can fly is a tractor," he added with a loud laugh. Sam said, "Mine flies a semi. They go higher." and a lot of joking began back and forth.

"Did you ever get to steer?" Ernie asked Stevie.

"Oh—once, for a minute. He was going to teach me some more, when I'm older—like Nels. He *was* teaching Nels. But I guess . . . I mean, he's moved to Millerton now."

Ernie didn't ask how come, or anything. He just turned back to the carburetor he and Bob were working on, saying, "Bet you miss him."

"Yeah," Stevie murmured. But not as much as Nels does, he thought. Nels had always been their dad's favorite, maybe just because he was oldest, or because he was named after him or something. Not that Dad *called* Nels "Nels"—he always said it was too much like talking to himself. He mostly called him Skipper, or just Skip. But he was always teaching Nels something, like chess, or the distances to stars, that Stevie was still too young for. Anyhow, I'm not as good at it as Nels, Stevie thought honestly. All that math stuff.

"Here, hold these, kid," said Bob surprisingly. It was always surprising when Bob said anything. Stevie turned to find a smudgy hand held out to him, with four little screws in the hollow of the palm. "Hang on. Don't drop 'em."

So Stevie had hung onto them, so tightly he'd had to pluck them out of his own palm one by one when Bob asked for them back, and they'd left little itchy red marks. After that, he often held things for Bob, or pulled hard on wires when Bob told him to, or handed him tools. He liked that; it was neat. He did not like it so well when some of the others began sending him on errands—around back of the school to find a scrap of board, or way back down the road past the Inn to Ernie's house to get a different wrench, or to the house just back of the Inn (he had to use the path through the jungly lilacs) to see what was keeping Sam's brother. In fact, he began to be privately grateful for Aunt Ruth's command to go no farther than the school; without that, he'd have spent half his time pedaling clear to the village, and the other half pedaling back.

On the whole, though, he considered it a fair exchange—a few errands and cookies in return for toleration from the boys. It didn't really matter how his time was spent, he always had more of it, hours and hours left over every day. His beetle cage idea hadn't worked. The beetles died. Stevie thought maybe they didn't have enough air, or didn't like those little bare styrofoam compartments. Or maybe he didn't give them the right kind of food—but he didn't know the right kind for each one, and it was no help at all that the book had finally arrived, because Nels was never around to look things up in it. It was one of those hard books, with a lot of Latin names and stuff in parentheses; it never just came out and *said* things, like what to feed click beetles. Nels always used to find out from it whatever they wanted; he knew how to use it. But since that awful morning after the peacock, Stevie didn't ask Nels things like that—or anything at all. He was never going to hang around Nels's neck again, not if he lived a hundred years.

That was ten days or so ago now—that peacock time. It seemed like years and years. Nels was like somebody else now, somebody none of them knew very well. They didn't even talk about it any more, or try to pester him. It wasn't any use. Stevie wondered what their mother would do when she saw Nels—when the summer ended and they all went home. Maybe it was just Nels's chrysalis and there wasn't anything to do, except wait for the beautiful butterfly. Stevie felt strongly that he would far prefer the old ordinary caterpillar-Nels he'd known all his life, but then nobody was asking him what he preferred, and probably nobody would listen if he told them at the top of his voice.

Nobody had said one word about his birthday, either. And it was tomorrow.

They've just forgotten it, you can't really blame them, Stevie told himself as he made a wide sweeping curve into the school's driveway. He'd thought Rory and Jenny might remember, but without Nels to remind them they hadn't. Aunt Ruth and Uncle Fred probably didn't even know. Nobody is trying to be mean, Stevie told himself again. It's just not important to anybody but me. He'd been telling himself this for a week now, and though it didn't make him feel any better, it had the stony, honest ring of truth, and so kept him from feeling any worse. He'd thought of mentioning it, just casually. He'd even tried to. But he couldn't get himself to do it. If people forgot things like birthdays, or didn't know about them, then that was just the way it had to be.

Mommie *really* won't forget though, Stevie thought as he swung off his bike on the far side of the jungle gym and kicked the stand into place. She'll send me something in the mail. Only not the watch, I bet. Nobody'll remember it's my year for a watch, so I mustn't expect one.

He took the box of vanilla wafers out of his basket and glanced uneasily toward the boys. He hoped there were a lot of cookies in this box. Holding it more or less behind him, he wandered over toward the minibike Bob was tinkering with and joined the group around it. Ernie glanced up and said, "Hi, kid," with an absent-minded smile. Two or three others turned, saw who it was, and turned back without saying anything. They were all watching closely as Bob did something delicate to the minibike's motor. It gave Stevie a chance to count them. Only twelve—thirteen, counting himself. There were bound to be more than thirteen cookies in a box this size.

Bob finished his job, and the tense group around him loosened and began talking and moving back, and Stevie had to jump to get out of the way. The boy whose bike it was got on it, and gunned the motor a few times while everybody shouted comments over the racket, then that boy and one of the others roared off across the playground and out the drive. So that left eleven. Stevie glanced hopefully around, but nobody else was leaving, and just then Wally hailed him from the direction of the swings.

"Hey, over here, over here! Don't let those guys eat 'em all up before we get a chance."

"I haven't even opened them yet," Stevie explained, hurriedly working at the box, but Wally was already walking toward him with Lloyd and Sam, and one of the others plucked the box from his hands and got it open, and it began to circulate around.

"Thanks, kid," Ernie said, and Bob nodded to Stevie as his hand dipped in, but Lloyd said, "Hey, it's a different kind," and somebody else said, "Yuck, what did you bring these dry things for, we'll need a gallon of water."

"I heard they put sawdust in these things," said somebody else. "No fooling. I really heard that."

"Better bring some Cokes tomorrow," Sam told Stevie. "Or ginger ale. Hey, how about a gallon of grape juice? That's what I like, grape juice."

"I don't think I could carry it on my bike," Stevie protested. "Anyhow, I don't think Aunt Ruth would let me have it. She—"

"Grape juice okay with you, Wally?" Sam was saying. "Hey, you guys—would you rather have grape juice or ginger ale tomorrow? The kid here's gonna bring us a whole gallon, maybe two, aren't you, kid?"

"No, *honest*!" Stevie knew Sam was only going on and on to be funny and wouldn't really expect any gallon of anything, but he kept nervously picturing six-packs of this and big jugs of that, none of them fitting into his bike basket. I wish I didn't have all this to worry about, he thought, suddenly feeling tired enough to go to sleep.

He put his finger in the ear next to Sam, and in the other ear heard Ernie saying, "Well, what time would we have to leave here, then?"

"Maybe nine-thirty, ten," Bob answered.

"There's a bus at nine-fifty, goes straight to Salem," said somebody. "Hey, Wally—hey, you guys. Meetcha at the bus stop tomorrow, instead of here. For that bike show, if you're going."

There was a chorus of agreement, questions about fares and schedules. Stevie grasped only the dismaying essential point. "You mean you're not even going to *come* tomorrow morning? Nobody'll be here?"

"What's the matter, punk?" Ernie said with a laugh. "That ought to suit you fine. You can have the swings all to yourself."

"But—it's my birthday," Stevie blurted, and immediately was stunned at himself. Why did I tell them? he thought incredulously. Why did I tell *them*?

Sam was already making a joke of it. "Hey, no *kidding*?" he shouted, eyes wide in his sunburned face. "Hey, listen, you guys, d'ja hear that? We can't go to that dumb bike show on a national holiday!"

"What national holiday?" demanded somebody who hadn't been listening.

"The kid's birthday, here! Hey, man! Why, we nearly missed the boat! You shoulda *told* us, kid! Why, we nearly went and—"

"Oh, shut up, Sam," Ernie told him. "How old are you going to be, Stevie?"

"Ten," muttered Stevie, staring at a fingernail. If it had been anybody but Ernie he wouldn't have answered. Just yesterday that two-digit 10, so much more impressive than 9 or 8, had seemed exciting, almost awesome—a milestone on the very border of the grown-up world. Now all at once ten seemed just a kid number; he was even unimpressed himself. Ernie said something friendly, and Bob did too, but Stevie scarcely heard them. He felt ashamed and miserable, as if he'd broken a promise or something. Why did I have to tell *them*? he kept thinking. It was private. Mine.

"You gonna have a party?" Wally asked him.

"No."

"No? How come? Guess we'll have to throw a party for you."

"Yeah! You bring the refreshments!" put in Sam with a bark of laughter.

"No, listen. Why don't we?" Wally turned to the others. "We could just come down here a little early tomorrow, before we catch the bus. Give the kid a ride on a real bike or something."

"Sure! Okay," said Ernie, and several voices agreed, though a couple more grumbled.

"Ah, come on, it's his birthday," Wally told one of the grumblers. "Don't be a drizzle-poop. Meetcha here like always, kid, okay? Only a little early, 'cause we gotta take off."

"Can you make it by nine-fifteen?" Ernie asked Stevie.

"Yeah. Sure. I can get here by nine o'clock." Stevie was staring from one to the other of them, feeling his ears get hot and then his cheeks, and a wonderful astonishment creep through him. "You mean really?" he added, just in case.

"Yeah, really," Bob told him, and that made it certain.

"I will bring refreshments!" Stevie burst out recklessly. "I'll bring—ice cream bars!"

There was a general laugh, and Ernie told him not to strain himself, and Sam said he was only kidding about the refreshments. But Stevie had already promised himself, silently but fervently, that he'd bring ice cream bars or bust.

And then they started talking about the bike show, and Ernie went home, and the day began to get more like other days. They mostly forgot about Stevie until somebody wanted him to ride back down the road and into Gruber's lane to Sam's house, to get a racing car magazine. He went willingly, but the happy astonishment was gradually turning into one large, uneasy question: how was he ever going to convince Aunt Ruth that he needed a dozen ice cream bars?

VI

THE AWFUL BIRTHDAY

NELS AWOKE to a gusty, sunny day, and the hot, dry climate of eastern Oregon brought across the mountains by a shift of wind. Yesterday he'd needed a sweater, as he did more often than not, until nearly noon. But this morning even the light covers seemed oppressive. He kicked them back, his mind already on the spaceship. Today he must bring the foil, and a detour to the store meant some changes in his customary smooth disappearance routine, as well as a plausible excuse for needing foil. He planned it all carefully as he dressed, worked out a couple of alternative escape routes in case of emergency, and after breakfast went directly to his room, got his allowance from the dresser drawer, and sat down to wait for everybody to start following the usual patterns.

And then, of course, everybody did something quite different. Stevie never came upstairs at all after breakfast, but disappeared somewhere himself, most conveniently. Rory and Jenny didn't go outdoors but came upstairs together, arguing heatedly about something involving string and telephones, went straight to their own room and started shouting out their west window to Maureen, who was apparently on the ground below. This was convenient too; as long as Nels could hear them, he could tell precisely where they were.

A glance at his watch told him the store was officially open. He waited no longer, but walked straight down the hall to the main stair, and with only a glance toward the sound of high-pitched discussion from the west wing, trotted rapidly down the steps and around the newel-post to launch himself at the store's open doorway.

And out of the doorway came Stevie, rushing away from the store as Nels rushed in. They collided hard enough to make them both stagger, and to send a cascade of loosely wrapped objects spurting from the flimsy box in Stevie's arms. The shock of impact—and of the old sore guilt—was followed by the far more shattering one of Stevie's outcry—a wail so charged with dismay that it drove everything else from Nels's mind.

"What's wrong?" he gasped, instinctively trying to catch the collapsing box, and being repelled with force.

"Nothing's wrong!" Stevie yelled, in a strangled voice. "Nothing, nothing, get away and leave me alone, why d'you have to turn up *now* and spoil it all?"

Shrinking under the sudden attack, Nels stared uncomprehendingly at the objects scattered on the floor, then bent to pick one up. "Ice cream bars? Where are you going with so many ice cream bars?"

"Never mind! It's none of your business—" Stevie dropped to his knees and began frantically trying to scoop the bars back into the box—without much success, as they kept slithering out of their papers and clattering back to the floor. Automatically Nels bent to help him, only to be met with a violent shove, and a choked, "Keep away!"

"Well, I was only—wanting to help." Nels was still struggling with confusion, trying to get his brain to work. "Where did you get all those things, anyway?" he asked in bewilderment.

"That's what I'd like to know," said Aunt Ruth's voice behind them, ominously level.

"Oh, *gol*—" wailed Stevie, and sat all the way down with a despairing thump, the box half off and half on his knees, and the bars sliding out of it, unheeded.

"Don't cry," Nels began uneasily, but Stevie was already

crying—howling—head thrown back, hands over his face, shoulders drawn up in a frenzy of misery and defeat. For a minute Nels longed to run—just cut and run, get out, get away—but he somehow kept from doing it.

"My conscience, child!" Aunt Ruth began to sound alarmed. "What ails you? Stevie, my dear! What is it?"

"My oh me! What's the trouble out there? Somebody hurt himself?" demanded Uncle Fred, hobbling as quickly as he could across the store.

"Stevie, stop! *Please*!" Nels dropped to his knees beside Stevie and tried to pull his hands away. "It'll be okay, just tell us what's the matter—I'll help you—"

He continued to plead, in vain. Uncle Fred arrived; Aunt Ruth alternated between answering his questions and asking agitated ones of her own. Rory and Jenny clattered down to the landing, eyes wide, piping voices demanding to know what happened to Stevie and who gave him all those ice cream bars.

And suddenly Stevie raised a bright pink, tear-ravaged face and cried out, "*Nobody* gave them to me. I just took them. Gol, I *stole* them—oh, Uncle Fred, I'm so sorry, I'll pay you back, honest I will—"

"Why, whatever is the child . . . *Stole* them?" Aunt Ruth gasped. "Stevie Anderson, do you mean to tell me—"

"Now, Ruth, now Ruth. Easy does it. Old Timer, listen. Now it's all right. Don't you go fretting about . . ."

"Yes, I will fret. And I'll pay it all back," Stevie choked. "Every bit. There's twelve of them—a whole box . . . and just look at them, now they're all mashed up and ruined and . . . oh, *gol*."

"Now, now, don't start again. Oh, you're so hot." Gently Aunt Ruth pulled him to his feet and dabbed at his flushed face with her handkerchief. "It's no great crime, I suppose. But why on earth—? I wish you'd tell us *why* you ever thought of such a thing. Child, you'd have been sick, eating twelve whole ice cream—"

"I wasn't going to eat them, they were for my friends!" Stevie swung around to Nels, eyes filling again. "They were for my *birthday* party. And you don't need to tell me it was dumb because I know it. So just shut up!"

Nels wasn't trying to tell him anything. His mouth had opened, but his mind had gone blank, the first shocked surprise changing to simple disbelief. Today couldn't be Stevie's birthday. *I'd have remembered,* he assured himself. He had never once forgotten, not once in Stevie's life. Why, he could almost remember the *birth* day, and Gram staying with him and his mother leaving. He certainly remembered the day she came home again, because Dad had let him hold the limp, heavy little blanketed bundle that they said was Stevie, on his lap for a moment. The baby had stared sort of cross-eyed at him and waved a frantic, quivering fist, and his heart had turned right over. And never once since had he forgotten August twenty-first.

"I didn't forget," he said, suddenly aware that he was shivering, and feeling a strange sensation on his scalp, as if all his hairs were lifting. "It can't be August twenty-first yet."

"It is. And you did forget," said Stevie. "Everybody forgot," he added fairly.

"*I* didn't!" Rory protested. "I mean, I didn't even *know*, so how could I forget? Nels always tells us."

"Yeah, Nels is supposed to tell us!" Jenny agreed. She turned an accusing look on Nels. "He never said a word, so how were we supposed to—"

"Okay, okay, I'm sorry," Nels cried, trying futilely to stem the sick flood of remorse that washed over him and through him. Everybody was talking now—the aunt and uncle in astonished tones, demanding why nobody had told them, why on earth Stevie's mommie hadn't let them know, why Nels hadn't said something. "I'm *sorry*," he kept saying, as he struggled to get his wits together. Could two whole weeks have gone by since that—peacock? He realized that he had no idea at all. Today might be any date, any day of the week; he could find no landmarks in the stream of time just past. "I'm sorry, Stevie," he repeated, forcing himself to meet Stevie's eyes. "I wouldn't have forgotten your *birthday*—I just didn't notice the date, I guess."

"That's okay," Stevie mumbled. He turned his back.

Aunt Ruth said, "Well, never you mind, the day's not over. There'll be a little party for you here tonight—at least something special for supper, and a cake. I'll go this minute and talk to Alice. If I'd just *known* a little earlier . . ."

She started off down the hall, Rory and Jenny drawn after her like iron filings after a magnet, asking questions in piercing whispers. Uncle Fred had noticed a customer and was hastily shuffling and tapping his way back into the store, tossing a "Happy Birthday, Old Timer," over his shoulder.

And I've got to leave too, Nels thought in sudden dismay, I haven't even got the foil, and I'm late, late . . .

But he couldn't leave yet—not feeling like this. Not without making it up somehow to Stevie, doing something. At least *saying* something. "Stevie?" he said, groping for words of apology, or for a better idea, wishing Stevie would turn around.

"Yeah, what?" said Stevie.

"Did you . . . say you were going to a party or something? With your friends?"

"No. That's all off now. They're gone."

"Gone? But—are you sure?"

"Yeah. The bus already left."

He seemed so sure that Nels was brought to a standstill, especially since he wasn't at all certain what they were talking about—what friends, what bus, what party—and he was suddenly feeling the strangeness of knowing so little about Stevie's life. As if I'd been away, Nels thought. Or sick or something . . . His mind shied away; he said hastily, "Stevie? Listen. About your friends—"

"Oh, forget it, it doesn't matter." Stevie turned wearily to face him. "They're not really my friends. I just sort of know them."

"But—who are they?"

"Oh . . . those big guys. You know."

"Down at the playground?" Nels said, astonished.

"Yeah."

"But . . ." But they're lots too old for him! Nels thought in dismay. They must be just teasing him or something. "Listen, Stevie, those big kids—"

"I know! You don't need to tell me. Anyway it's all over. You don't think I'd go down there again after I never showed up with the ice cream bars!"

"I don't get why you had to bring the ice cream anyhow, when it was your own—"

"Oh, let's not talk about it!" Stevie cried. Head down, hands jammed in pockets, he started for the back garden, walking fast. Nels followed him out the French doors into the gusty hot wind. It was as if he couldn't prevent himself, as if something terrible would happen if he left Stevie now.

"Stevie, wait. Please don't just go off feeling bad."

"Well, gol, how can I help how I feel?" Stevie flung a harassed glance over his shoulder. "You think I *want* to feel some way special? I don't even *want* it to be my birthday." He stopped by the crumbling birdbath. "I wish it was *next year*, that's what I wish."

"Next year! Why?" Nels was curling into a hard, tight ball inside at the very thought of next year.

"I don't know. Because *this* year would be over, I guess. Let's not talk about it any more."

"Okay," Nels muttered. But he had to ask one thing. "Didn't Mommie send you a present?"

"No."

Nels felt suddenly short of breath, as if somebody had punched him in the ribs. "She will!" he rushed on, trying to talk away the sensation. "She's bound to—there's still today's mail, after lunch. Dad will, too. He might be late—you know how Dad is—and with nobody to remind him . . . I mean, actually it's easy to—to sort of forget what day it is—though I'm not saying—"

"Oh, shut up, *please*. I don't want to keep on talking about it." Stevie started walking again, around the birdbath, across the weed-grown rose garden. The wind kept worrying the lilacs beyond, turning their leaves, then releasing them.

"All right, I'll quit. I promise." Nels wondered if he had ever felt as miserable, as guilty, as apprehensive. His mind flashed to the General's room; Alan would be getting tired of waiting. Maybe he was already gone—or deciding to go soon, looking at his watch and giving Nels five more minutes . . . No, he'll wait for me, please let him wait for me, Nels thought, still following Stevie as if tied to him. He could feel the sun beating down on the top of his head. "Where are you *going*?" he asked in near exasperation.

"I don't know." Stevie came to a halt beside the lilacs as if his steam had run out. "Nowhere, I guess. I used to always go to the school grounds, but . . . I don't know," he repeated in a muddled voice. He turned bleak blue eyes to search Nels's face. "Where do you go all the time?" he said. "Not that you'd tell me."

And Nels heard himself saying, "How do you know I wouldn't? What if—what if I did?"

There was silence, as he gradually grasped the import of his own words. Stevie's eyes had widened.

"You mean you would?" he whispered.

Slowly, Nels nodded, feeling himself go still inside. But it was the right answer, he knew it—it would make everything quit hurting. He *would* tell Stevie. This time he wouldn't let Alan stop him. "I *will*," he promised. "I wanted to before. Honest. But I just—couldn't."

"And now you can?"

"Yes. I mean—anyway I *will*. Only first I have to—go away for a minute. I have to tell somebody," Nels explained hastily as Stevie's face changed, and the light went out of his eyes. "I'll come back. *Truly*."

"Yeah, okay." Stevie said resignedly. He turned away.

Nels's heart was thumping and sore, like some lead thing dragging at him. "I know you don't believe me. But this time I really will, I promise on my word of honor!" He glanced at his watch. So *late*. Nearly ten o'clock. "It may take me a little while. But don't worry, see? I'll come back by lunchtime, and I'll have a big surprise."

"Nels, wait! Just stay here now. Instead. I'd rather, honest. I don't want the surprise. I don't even want to know—anything."

"But it's great, Stevie! A really great secret—and you'll be in on it too. Of course, *you've* got to promise to keep it then. You mustn't tell *anybody* . . . listen, I have to go now or it won't—work. Don't watch me or try to follow me, okay? Just this one more time. And don't mention I'm going any place special. I'll come back, *cross my heart*, before noon."

Stevie didn't answer. When Nels glanced back from the French doors he was still standing there, again facing the wind-ruffled lilacs, his thumbs in his pockets, his towhead like metal in the sun.

But it'll be all right, Nels thought as he flew toward the

stairway. He'll find out it's true this time, then he'll believe me again—and anyway it'll be great to have him up there too! Wait till he sees the ship—Nels paused, halfway up the stairs, wiping the sweat from his upper lip, remembering the foil. No, never mind that now, he thought, rushing on again. I'll have enough to do just talking Alan into this . . . later we can work on the ship again. Stevie can help! He's good with his hands. I'll tell Alan that. And I'll tell him . . .

But Alan had said it was impossible to include Stevie.

What did he *mean* by "impossible"? Nels thought. He was hurrying along the upstairs hall toward the screen—but not running now, because he was feeling so queer and breathless. It's got to be possible. Stevie's got to share. I'll tell Alan that. Either we let Stevie in or—or I'll quit coming. And that's the way it's got to *be*.

He had reached the east wing passage. And suddenly he could go no further; he sagged against the wall, his shoulder sliding a little on the dark-varnished paneling, his legs achy and weak beneath him. *Quit coming*. Did he mean that? It was an ultimatum. What if Alan simply shrugged and said, "So okay, quit!" Or if it turned out to be literally, physically impossible to let Stevie in? Then would he mean it still? Would he give up the spaceship—and the ciphers and the printing press and the long busy days—give up Alan's father and mother—and *Alan*—and the warm, safe happiness of the tower? Could he bear that?

I'll have to, Nels thought, forcing his legs to hold him, carry him forward again. I'll just have to. Because I can't bear this.

He reached the door of the General's room, and with a burst of relief saw Alan turn from the window. Without speaking or trying to, Nels kept going, half staggering, toward the bookcase, with Alan close behind. And then they were there at last, tumbling into the shadowy sanctuary, and with a feeling of blessed escape, blessed safety, Nels seized the coat hook and pulled hard.

And he heard the *click*, clear and sharp beside his ear, as the latch went home.

FOR A SECOND he couldn't move, or even understand what he had done. Then, unbelieving, he tried to open the door again, fumbled for the hook and tugged and twisted it to no effect. With growing uneasiness he turned to stare blindly behind him, where Alan must be. "It locked! I didn't mean . . . help me, can't you? You go in and out all the time, you know how to open it!"

"Not when you've latched it yourself," said Alan's voice.

"But I didn't mean to! I want it open, like always, please don't tease me! Not today! I—" There was no response. Suddenly angry and frightened, Nels hurled himself at the door again, drove his shoulder against it over and over, beat at it and kicked it, flung his whole weight upon its handle, turned himself into a battering ram—and finally sank hot and panting against it, nursing his sore shoulder. In the silence, he realized that Alan was laughing—a full, rich laugh of triumph and pure pleasure. Incredulously Nels turned toward the sound—so familiar, at this moment so chilling. "Why are you *laughing*?" he whispered.

"Well, you act so funny! Besides, I'm glad. Now you live here too."

"I don't! I don't!" Nels shouted. With a thrill of terror he stared through the darkness at Alan, again attacked the door with furious blows and kicks.

"Oh, what are you making such a rumpus for?" Alan said in the impatient, half-scornful tone that so often had brought Nels around to a new point of view. "This was bound to happen, sooner or later. So now you can stay."

"But I can't! I *can't* stay here. I won't!"

"Well, you'll have to. You're here most of the time anyhow, so what's the difference?"

"What's the *difference*?" There were so many differences, such vast and unimaginable differences between being prisoner and being free, that it was no use even starting on them. "Oh, why won't you help me?" Nels burst out. "I've got to get out of here pretty soon, I told Stevie I'd come back, I promised!"

"What's Stevie got to do with it?"

Nels's anger exploded. "Everything! He's got everything to do with it! He's my brother, can't you understand that? And I promised! And it's his *birthday*. Don't you understand at all? . . . Don't you even care?"

"About Stevie? No," Alan said.

In the silence, Nels absorbed the flat indifference of Alan's tone. A shiver ran through him; his eyes felt stretched from peering blindly through the darkness. "Well, don't you care about me?" he asked.

There was no direct answer this time, only Alan's slightly exasperated sigh, and his usual, "Nels, quit worrying! Haven't I just been saying I want you to stay, and I'm glad, and everything?"

But the answer, again, was *no*. Nels suddenly knew that. "You only care about what you want," he whispered. His voice was shaking; he had begun to shake all over, as he pressed back against the door and away from Alan. "I thought you were my friend. But you don't really care about anybody—about anything—just yourself! You're a horrible person!"

"Oh—dummy—everybody's that way."

"They're not! I'm not!"

"Then why are you here? Instead of downstairs with your precious Stevie or something? You came because *you* wanted to, didn't you? You latched that door because you wanted to, too. —Oh, yes you did!" Alan's voice rose fiercely over Nels's protests. "I played fair—I warned you lots of times. I never once touched the door."

"But you—you—I only—" The denials choked Nels; the truth was choking him—the truth in Alan's words. But it wasn't the whole truth—it wasn't the *real* truth, surely? Nels questioned himself wildly: *I can't be like that? Can I?* He cried, "You're twisting everything! And you're lying, too. It's not like that!"

"Oh—come on, Nels." Alan's voice was suddenly coaxing and relaxed. "You've got yourself all bent out of shape—cool off, why don't you? Come on up and let's work on the spaceship. Good old "Agmet". It doesn't matter about the foil, I found out Mom had some. We can start putting that on, and after a while—"

"No. No. *No*." Nels knew only enough to resist, to fear the longing for peace and comfort that was beginning to beckon like a rainbow.

"Oh, come *on*. Mom's making raisin cake—and Dad stayed home today just specially to help us. Maybe later I can figure out how to get that door unlatched again. I'll try to, honest."

"No . . ." And then Nels saw what to do. Alan's parents—they would understand, and sympathize. They had before. They'd make Alan let him go. "Okay," he said abruptly. "I'll come. But only if I can see your mom and dad. Right *now*."

"Well, sure. Any time you like. Let's go."

The crack of light appeared behind Alan, widened swiftly as he stepped aside. Nels's rush carried him straight past, through the sunlit blur of color that was the room beyond, up the spiral stair in the corner. Alan's footsteps rang behind his on the iron treads. The six-sided hall, usually dim and mysterious, was flooded with daylight today. Every door was open. As Nels halted in surprise, Alan's dad appeared from the living room carrying the spaceship plans, and Alan's mother from the kitchen, with a plate of golden cake slices.

"Oh, good!" she cried. "It's just out of the oven. I thought you'd be here soon. Come right in to the table—"

"No, wait! Wait, I can't!" Nels put his hands to fend off the plate she was offering him. "Please—I have to go back downstairs right away—it's my brother's birthday—and the door locked somehow and Alan won't open it . . ." He broke off, anxiously scanning her face, which still smiled a bright, warm, uncomprehending smile, while she stood still extending the plate. "Please—listen—" With a little thrill of fear, Nels swung toward Alan's father. "*Please.* I *have* to get out of here. Make Alan help me!" Alan's father stood smiling, leaning kindly toward him, holding the ship plans in his hand. "Can't you hear me?" Nels cried—then shouted, then screamed. "Can't you hear me? Can't you *hear*?"

They never moved or answered. They stood like smiling wax figures, unchangeable—like statues of Parenthood. And gradually, while Nels still stared at them, they faded away, leaving nothing but empty sunlight, and empty rooms. When they were quite gone, Alan laughed. The sound was pure amusement—and pure malice. It ran through Nels like ice water. He transferred his stare to Alan, who was leaning in his own doorway, real as ever.

"Come on in," he said. "My room's the same as always. We can work on the ship by ourselves."

"I won't. I'll never do anything you say again. Not ever," Nels whispered. He couldn't quit staring at Alan—couldn't believe he looked just the same, with his dark hair, his red sleeveless sweater, his snub nose and wide, curved mouth. "*All this time*. All fake and phoney. Everything! Just one big fraud." He backed up a step, feeling sick. "You're a horrible, hateful person. And I hate you!"

"Oh, you'll get over it."

"I'll die first!" gasped Nels. He couldn't bear to look at Alan another second. Whirling, he plunged down the iron steps—expecting them to vanish under him any second—stumbled across the room he had never yet seen and now suddenly feared as he had never feared anything, and flung himself headlong into the bookcase-closet. Behind him the opening narrowed at once to a rainbow-colored crack, and he was in darkness—now welcome, now an enfolding refuge. Alan had not followed him down; he felt reasonably sure of that. No shadow crossed the rainbow crack; no slightest sound came from that room beyond—or from anywhere else. He was alone here, with his ragged breathing. He groped away from the crack, as far as the narrow space would allow, until his back was pressed flat against the familiar bookcase door. If it would not open, at least it would not vanish. It was real and solid—one with the solid, ordinary bookcase on the other side, which looked out on an ordinary, solid room.

But that might explain it, thought Nels, pressing harder against the back of the door as he felt himself start to shiver all over. It would explain, maybe, why the door won't open. Maybe I closed the door on the Present. Maybe, *here*, it's still fifty years ago. Maybe fifty years ago there wasn't any door there—just solid wall. And maybe that's why nobody could hear me pounding and yelling awhile ago—because there *isn't anybody there.*

He was shaking uncontrollably now, and panic rose up in him like a sob and spilled over into another frenzied attack upon the door, with fists and feet and fingernails and even his head, while he burst his throat with shouting, then storming, then mere incoherent screaming, until at last he collapsed into a sweaty, exhausted heap on the dusty floor. It was his head hurting sharply, and the pain of a couple of broken fingernails, that brought him out of his fog of fear and back to some grasp on reality. *I mustn't do that*! he thought—it was the only clear thought he could summon, and he clung to it grimly as he sat gasping and fighting to get himself under control. *I mustn't scream, I mustn't pound, I must be calm.*

Then he heard Alan's voice—from a little distance, as if he were calling from the top of the iron stairs. "Hey, Nels! It's no good doing all that, you know. Honest. Come on back up."

I'll die first, Nels told him silently. He sat tense and still, ears strained for the first footfall on an iron tread. But none sounded. Instead, Alan's voice came again, from the same distance.

"Nels? You must be getting awful hot in that place. I've got some lemonade up here . . . Nels! Are you okay? . . . Hey, aren't you going to answer?"

No. I'm not going to answer you. Ever again.

"Oh, all right, be stubborn, then." It was the old bored, impatient tone. "But you're just wasting good building time. I'll start putting the foil on by myself." The voice faded, as if Alan had turned away from the stairs.

Nels sat motionless, listening, waiting. When nothing further happened, he gradually relaxed, cautiously changing the cramped position of his legs. He had expected Alan to come down after him—especially when he got no answer. Maybe, he speculated, he *can't* come after me. Maybe now he's caught on his side of some time-barrier, just as I'm caught here. So maybe—No. *Forget* the time theory. I just made that up.

Alan's voice suddenly called again, faint, then louder, as if he had come out of his room into the six-sided hall to shout down the stairs. "Nels? Aren't you ever going to cut out moping and come help me with this? Come *on*, won't you *please*? I don't know how it's supposed to go. Did you want the strips of this foil to go up and down, or round the thing horizontally? . . . Nels? . . . Well, I'll go on and put them up and down, then—shiny side out."

No, that's wrong! Nels clamped his lips tight to keep from saying it aloud. Don't answer, don't answer, he warned himself.

"Nels, *please* come on, it's your ship really, and I'm bound to get it all fouled up . . . In fact I'll bust it on purpose!" the voice was suddenly spiteful.

Go ahead, Nels told it silently. *Go right ahead*.

There was a sound of baffled anger, then a fading, "Have it your way!"

I will, Nels thought. There was nothing further from above.

He can't come down, Nels reassured himself. Not if I won't answer him. I could still go up there—and that's what he's trying to get me to do, but I won't. I will not ever again. I'll die first.

It occurred to Nels, as he turned at last away from the rainbow-colored crack and peered around him in the stuffy darkness, that he might, quite literally, die first—die right here. How long could a person live in a place about four feet by four feet by six feet high, without air or light or water?

Don't think about that, he told himself sharply, as he felt the clutch of panic like fingers on his throat. He must *not* lose control again. He must not batter at the door or shout, it didn't work. For some reason he didn't understand, nobody could hear him. *Why*? he thought. Oh, why, *why* can't they, when the General's room is right above the kitchen, and somebody's always in the kitchen, and Alice used to hear the General all the time, just walking up and down? Unless—

No. He must not start believing in that empty, house of thirty years ago, either. *I just made that up. Admit it!* But there *was* some reason why, there must be . . . With an effort, Nels summoned up the mental jigsaw he had once pieced together, of the whole east wing and how the rooms went together. And then he saw the reason: this closet was *not* over the kitchen. It was over the pantry—a place lined with cupboards and thus accoustically dead—what's more, it was on the dining room side of the pantry, probably just above the shelves full of old hotel tablecloths and napkins. A perfect soundproofing.

For a quailing moment, he tried to reject it. He had often heard kitchen sounds in here, hadn't he? No. Only out in the General's room—or when he opened the bookcase wide to go downstairs. Could he hear a single sound from downstairs now? No. So naturally they couldn't hear him . . . at least it *was* natural—and any ordinary, light-of-day reason was preferable to that nightmarish empty house. Nels stood up and felt all around the crack that proved the door was not a solid wall . . . groped in the left-hand corner until his fingers closed on the yardstick he had seen the very first time he had peered inside.

It is that same place, he told himself firmly; the door has got locked, that's all. *Sometime, somebody will open it*. They'll miss me—sooner or later, even if it's tomorrow. And they'll look everywhere, even here.

But nobody knew the bookcase opened.

I'll tell them! I'll hear them come searching, and yell to them. They'll hear me easily *then*.

But if he shouldn't hear them come? The heat was making him so drowsy. If he should fall asleep from it, from exhaustion, from lack of air? If he should be unconscious, or even—

It won't be that long! They'll know something's wrong—Stevie will. Stevie won't forget—I told him I'd be back before lunch.

And how many times had he told Stevie he'd be back before lunch?

Oh, let him believe me just one more time! Nels thought desperately.

He let his shaky legs go and fell on his knees, hugging himself, clenching his jaw and grimacing to squeeze back the flood of tears. He would *not* cry, that was stupid and it would only make him hotter and more miserable. He stripped off his shirt, sat down on the floor and leaned back against the side wall, forcibly composing himself to wait. He would *not* give in to drowsiness. And somebody would come. They *would*. Stevie would.

Oh, please, let him believe me just one more time.

STEVIE WAS just starting his seventeenth game of checkers with himself when the lunch bell rang. With relief he swept the black and red disks into their box, realizing he had been bored to distraction for an hour. How stupid could a person get, playing the same game sixteen times and then starting it again? He could have gone for a dozen bike rides, found innumerable beetles to watch, spent the whole morning helping the little kids string their telephone.

But—stupider and stupider—he hadn't been able to bring himself to leave the house, just in case Nels might try to find him. And naturally Nels hadn't showed up. So much for wonderful surprises. So much for promises.

Jenny came bursting in the front door and ran directly up the stairs, leaving the door swinging wide behind her.

"Hey, the bell rang for lunch!" Stevie called to her.

"I heard it! I'm going to wash my hands."

Stevie walked over and closed the door, and after a moment started for the little washroom across the hall. Then he suddenly followed Jenny up the stairs instead, swung around the newel-post and ran down the hall to his own room. But Nels had not miraculously come back; there was no sign that he had been there. The astronomy book he had been leafing through early that morning lay open, just as he had left it, on the desk. There was even a light film of dust over the pages. For some reason that made a curious little chill run through Stevie.

Oh, don't be dumb! he told himself crossly, stalking over to slam the book. He nearly slammed the window shut too—that's where the dust was coming from; it always blew in when they had this hot east wind kind of weather. But without that breeze it would get suffocating in here. He left the window open and went downstairs.

Aunt Ruth was disposed to pass over Nels's absence from the lunch table in a sort of severe silence, as if he had been unpardonably rude. Nels was getting altogether too absent-minded lately, she said repressively when Jenny asked where he was. If he could not get to the table on time he must simply go without his lunch. That closed the subject. Only Stevie remained unsatisfied with the explanation, and that against all common sense, because nobody agreed more than he that Nels had got too absent-minded lately.

But this time he *promised*, Stevie kept thinking. He *really* felt bad about—the birthday and everything. I could tell. And he said word of honor, and cross his heart, and about the wonderful surprise, and that he'd wanted to tell me before. He wouldn't just *say* all that, would he?

The question hung around in Stevie's mind, refusing to be answered with either "yes" or "no," while he buttered a roll and didn't eat it, pushed his meat loaf around his plate, and decided he wasn't hungry. Maybe he hadn't heard Nels right. Maybe Nels had said right *after* lunch. He for sure had said not to mention anything to anybody.

But after lunch, when there was still no sign of Nels, Stevie put his vague uneasiness behind him and listened to common sense. By now it was perfectly plain that Nels had simply forgotten him again—forgotten all of them. Nels *would* just say all that. To get rid of me, thought Stevie, making himself face it. To get away. He doesn't want to be with me any more. So just get used to it.

In spite of the obvious truth of all this, he kept right on feeling, deep inside, that Nels should have come back by now, that something was peculiar. He couldn't get himself to leave the front hall, but dawdled around as if he were tied there, practicing walking on his hands or quietly *vrooming* his little Ferrari along the top of the old hotel reception desk, or just standing by the French doors staring out at the lilac jungle where Nels had said all that. He even asked a tentative question—cautiously, still mindful of Nels's instruction—of Aunt Ruth as she came past on one of her hurried trips between store and kitchen, carrying a box of frosting mix and a handful of lollipops. She couldn't understand why he was worried.

"Good gracious child, you know how Nels is, he'd forget his head if it weren't fastened on him! He'll be around by dinner-time, never you fear—probably long before that. He wouldn't miss your birthday dinner! Why don't you go play with Rory and Jenny? Get busy with something. Here—you can take these things to Alice for me, for a start. Now run along, find something to do!"

Stevie went, but Rory and Jenny had gone to Maureen's house as usual, and Alice was busy cooking; Stevie would never have talked to *her* about it anyhow. He went out and sat on the front steps.

At last the mail came, and things got a little better. There were two packages for him, brown paper on the outside and wonderful bright birthday wrappings within. Beginning to feel the sort of tingly, breathless way that was proper for a birthday, Stevie carefully unwrapped them, making the process last as long as possible. Neither package contained a watch. But it was almost as good, maybe even better, he assured himself, to have the new jackknife his father had sent (in a box that had looked heart-stoppingly like a watch box at first). It was a much bigger and more complicated knife than the old brass-handled one he had lost last summer, and had a nail file, bottle opener, leather punch and screw driver as well as three blades.

It was his mother who sent the really great thing, three things really. The first was a strong grocery carton—it was part of the birthday present—containing six pieces of wood cut to special lengths, a few nails, a roll each of plastic wrap, aluminum foil and tape, and a rectangle of wire screen. With it came a book, one with good plain sentences and plenty of illustrations, that told exactly how to put all this together to make an Insect Zoo, where you could keep live beetles and things to watch. To top off everything, she had sent a brand new insect net—the kind you bought at a store. It was as if she had been reading Stevie's mind.

With his new knife and a hammer borrowed from Uncle Fred, it took him just half an hour to turn his box into a sturdy cage with a screened top to let air in, a plastic-wrap window to watch through, and a lidlike door on top—that was how clear the book's instructions were. He spread layers of aluminum foil in the bottom as the book said, then carried his zoo across the road to get the layer of crumbly dirt that went over that—also some pebbles and chips for the beetles to hide under when they felt like it.

After that he walked on down the path and under the railroad trestle to Maureen's to show his presents to Jenny and Rory. He wished he could show them to Ernie and Bob too, but he knew he would never again go to the school playground—not after this morning. Most of all he longed to show them to Nels, to be starting off right now with him and the new net, to Parker's meadow. And suddenly not even the zoo seemed good any longer—not if he couldn't show it to Nels.

Where *was* Nels? The day seemed already twice as long as other days—maybe because of the heat and the restless wind. Heading back to the Inn, Stevie changed course abruptly and walked along the driveway beside the kitchen, staring up at those east windows as he went, meanwhile telling himself Nels couldn't be *there*, and not to be feeble-minded. But a moment later he was slipping up the back stairs anyway, his heart beginning to thump a little, steeling himself for the hateful sight of that room he had never gone near since the morning after the peacock night. Doggedly he squeezed behind the carved thing, went along the passage, made himself push open the half-closed door. But even before he looked in, he felt sure the room was empty. This time there was not even the feeling that there had been someone there an instant before. It was just an empty room.

Stevie opened his mouth—and closed it again. Even that other time, when he had *seen* Nels hurry in here only a moment before, calling had been useless. To call and get no answer just made you feel lonesomer.

Bitterly, feeling his throat knot up with disappointment, he left as quickly and silently as he had come, and retreated down the hall to his own room where he put the zoo aside and flung himself on his bed. Raising a hot, flushed face some time later, he sat up wearily and stripped off his jersey and undershirt. A cool bath might help some, and a thin, short-sleeved shirt. It was nearly four o'clock, and hotter than ever, in spite of the wind that was still blowing dust in on Nels's book. Stevie walked over and put the book in a drawer, swiping it off with his hand as he did so, then stood leaning on the desk and staring out the window at the empty, sun-baked road, wishing it would hurry and get cool again—wishing once more with all his heart that it was next year, and he was eleven. However that would feel, it couldn't be as bad as it had felt so far to be ten—and at least this worst of all birthdays would be behind him, forever.

At about five-thirty Rory and Jenny came straggling back from Maureen's, flushed and hot, irritable because the wind kept blowing and they were hungry. They were more inclined to sit on the front steps and bicker than to get ready for dinner, and Aunt Ruth sent Stevie out to remind them.

"Oh, yeah! Your birthday dinner!" said Rory, brightening. "I almost forgot again. We've got a present for you, too—haven't we, Jen?"

"Yeah," Jenny said with a sudden grin. Both of them began to giggle. "Aunt Ruth won't like it," Jenny added.

"No. Not at the dinner table," Rory agreed, with dancing eyes. "But *you* will," he told Stevie.

"Okay, but you better go on and take baths now, or you'll be late," Stevie told them. He had an idea the present was a beetle of some kind. He appreciated it, too. In fact, looking at the two of them sitting there in their rumpled T-shirts and stubby sneakers, Rory's blond head with its tumble of curls close to

Jenny's shiny brown one—Jenny's hair always looked as if it had been polished—Stevie felt an almost painful surge of love for both of them. As Rory whispered something that made them explode with laughter, Stevie actually felt tears starting to his eyes. What if he didn't have any Jenny and Rory, either? Not at all, not ever? Just imagine how lonesome that would be! "Go on, now," he said loudly, thinking, Why am I getting so mushy over them, anyway?—and knowing it was almost *dinner-time*, and still no sign of Nels, and by now he was feeling as if there was a volcano inside him that might erupt at any moment.

"Okay." Rory sighed, and got up reluctantly to go inside. "I don't see why we've got to take *baths,* though."

"You have to, too," Jenny told Stevie.

"I already did. Gol, can't you tell? Take a cool one, it feels good."

"Yeah, let's do! C'mon, Rory." Jenny disappeared inside, Rory hurrying after her saying, "I get to have the big sponge!"

Slowly Stevie followed. Neither one of them had said a word about Nels—maybe they didn't know he was gone. Or maybe they were so used to it by now they didn't really care. Nobody seemed to care. *Except me*, thought Stevie desperately. But he had said no more to Aunt Ruth about it—to anybody—and he wasn't going to if he could help it. Nels might wander in to dinner with that far-off look and not even remember he'd made any promise. Or else he *wouldn't*, and surely then, Stevie told himself, somebody else will notice he's gone!

He was beginning to feel unreal about the whole thing, as if he'd just made Nels up out of his own head, and nobody else knew there even was any such person. It was the way they *acted*, Stevie thought, getting up so abruptly from the game table that he came near sending his zoo box tumbling to the floor. As if Nels had just—blown away like smoke, and nobody would ever mention him again.

Aunt Ruth appeared suddenly from the dining room. "Stevie? Oh, there you are." She moved briskly toward the stairway. "Child-*ren*! Out of that tub now. Dinner in ten minutes! . . . Has Nels come downstairs yet?" she asked Stevie as she turned back.

"No," Stevie blurted. It came out like a hiccup—partly because it had waited so long on the tip of his tongue for somebody to ask that question, partly because a sort of gasp came with it.

"No? Well, my conscience, he'd better hurry too!" Aunt Ruth turned again to the stairwell. "Nels? Oh, Nels!"

"He's not upstairs!" Stevie got out. It was extraordinarily hard to say anything—as if he'd waited too long, and the words were all wedged together and tangled.

"You mean he hasn't even come back? Where is he?"

"I don't *know*. I don't *ever* know where he goes or why he goes, or—" Stevie was beginning to gulp and his eyes stung and there was a hard-knot pain in his throat, and he suddenly couldn't speak at all because his throat closed tight.

Aunt Ruth was staring at him, hurrying forward. "Stevie my *dear* . . . Now Stevie. It'll be all right. Just tell me what you mean. Is Nels at somebody else's house?"

"I don't *know*. He said he had to ask somebody. Before he could tell me the secret. But I don't know who, or—"

"Maybe one of the boys in your Sunday school class?"

"No, no, somebody *here*!"

"But child, there's nobody here except . . . You can't be talking about somebody in the Rooftop Realty? They—"

"No, no—I don't *know*. All I know is that he went away somewhere and he *promised* he'd come back—*before lunch*—and it's getting so *late*, and—

The tears burst forth in spite of all, and Stevie found himself gathered tightly to Aunt Ruth's chest. It was a thin, bony sort of chest, with a string of hard-edged beads running down and then up it like a rocky road because Aunt Ruth had dressed up for the birthday, but it felt comforting to Stevie anyhow. Just to get all that *said* had made him feel better—and to have somebody else finally talking about Nels and getting alarmed. He was sure Aunt Ruth was alarmed now—at least fully alert. The moment he got his tears choked back—and it was only a moment, because his throat had begun to untie—she pushed him far enough away to look into his face, and began to question him closely.

He did his best to answer, but he didn't know much. By the time Aunt Ruth had run out of questions, Rory and Jenny had come leaping down the stairs, with Uncle Fred, dressed in his Sunday suit, making his slow descent behind them, and Alice had appeared to summon them to the birthday dinner table. And in a moment everyone knew that Nels was missing, and in all their faces, Stevie saw alarm flaring up like little candle flames.

Jenny's turned rapidly to fright. "But where *is* Nels?" she said in a thin, quivering little voice. "I don't want Nels to be gone."

"It's okay, Jenny," Rory said, but his own eyes were wide, moving from Aunt Ruth to Uncle Fred to Alice and finally fixing on Stevie with discomforting intensity. "It'll be okay, won't it, Steve?"

"How do I know?" Stevie burst out. "You guys didn't even miss him," he added. It wasn't fair, and he knew it, but he couldn't help saying it. "You didn't even ask where he was!"

"Well, let's go *look* for him," Rory said. "Have you looked for him? What'f he got run over?" He swallowed hard. "What'f he climbed into an old refrigerator like those kids in the newspaper, and—"

"Now just shut up!" Stevie told him loudly. Rory's frightened face made him wild with fright himself, and Jenny was crying by now. "Nels wouldn't climb into any old refrigerator, dummy, d'you think he's *stupid*?"

"Children, hush." The grown-ups had been having a hurried consultation, and Aunt Ruth turned to them. "Now we're going to find Nels," she said firmly. "There's nothing to cry about, Jenny, we *will* find him, if we each do our part . . ." She began to send everybody here and there, to search in different places. Stevie's orders were search up and down the road on his bike, but it felt wrong, all wrong.

"Isn't anybody going to look here? Upstairs?" he asked uneasily.

"But you said you looked upstairs already!"

"Well, yes, I did, but—"

"Then we'd just waste time." Aunt Ruth spoke gently, but turned him toward the door as she did so. "Run on, now. Before it's dark."

She was already heading for the phone of the old reception desk, and the others had scattered. Stevie went out the back door for his bike, fighting his reluctance all the way. *This* felt like the waste of time. But he wanted to do his part. He pedaled into the driveway, gravel spurting as he made the turn. The wind was still blowing in little puffs, like an animal panting, and its breath was still warm. Ferry Road lay deserted, with the flat evening light making it look even emptier, and different somehow—like a turned-off television screen, or a clock that had stopped. It's because everybody's home eating supper, Stevie told himself uneasily. Maybe the road looks this way every evening when nobody's here to see.

Suddenly he made a wide U-turn and started back up the driveway. It wasn't dark yet—he'd go upstairs once more before he went down the road. Just one more try . . . He found himself pedaling quickly now, with a sense of release, of being headed in the right direction. It was as plain as if a voice at his elbow were whispering encouragement: *Good—you're getting warm now—warmer—* In the service yard, he let the bike clatter to the ground and lie there with one wheel spinning, as he hurried up the step to the back door. He could hear Aunt Ruth's voice from the passage—she was still talking on the reception desk phone. Silently, but no less urgently, he ran up the back stairs. The answer was up there, he knew it was—if it was anywhere.

Nobody was around. The upstairs hall looked like the road, as empty in the tired late light as if nobody had ever set foot there. Hot and trembly from his rush, Stevie slipped behind the screen and stood a second, puffing, staring down the little east passage. The voice was saying "Hot!" now, and he didn't even need it—he felt as if something inside him was attached to something inside that room, and was pulling and pulling.

Softly he walked down the passage and into the room. It was just as empty as before, and just as silent. But the inner voice was yelling, "Red hot! Scorching! Fire!" and suddenly he was yelling too. "Nels! Where are you? Nels!" He knew it was probably no use, but it was the only thing left to do, and he just kept doing it—crying, "Nels! Please, Nels! Nels!"

And then he hushed, with his heart stopped, thinking he had heard some sound—a thump, a . . . something. "*Nels*!" he gasped, as his heart started up again with a heavy pounding. "Nels! *Nels*!" A moment's waiting, his breath held—and it came again. A brief, weak thump, a sort of scuffling. This time he was sure he heard it, but not sure what it was or where it came from. "Where are you?" he cried. "Nels! Say something! Are you okay?"

"Here," said a tiny, muffled thread of a voice—but it was Nels's, he would have known it in the wilds of Manchuria, or at the bottom of the ocean. Eighteen thousand bricks lifted off his heart and he was no more earthbound than a feather.

"Where?" he sang out. "I'll help you, Nels, just tell me where you are!"

He heard the tiny thread of voice, but it was a moment before he could make out what Nels was saying, and he had to keep repeating, "What?" At last one desperate word came clearly: *Bookcase*.

"Bookcase?" Stevie said blankly, turning to stare at the built-in bookshelf on the other side of the room. He went over to it quickly, calling, "What d'you mean? What about the bookcase?"

Nels's voice came again, still a rasping whisper but clearer now, and with a note of all-out, last-chance effort in it that sent a little thrill of fright through Stevie.

"Stevie—listen. I'm *behind* the bookcase. It opens. But only from outside. *Don't pull it*. Push. Then let go. Try."

Swallowing, Stevie stepped close to the bookcase, pushed on one of the shelves, let go. Nothing happened. He tried again, harder, then turned a shoulder and slammed the whole weight of his body against it. "It doesn't work! I can't do it!" he cried, clutching his throbbing shoulder. "I'm trying, honest—I'll try some more so don't you worry—" He broke off, realizing that Nels was saying something. "What?"

". . . the *right side*. Not the middle. To your right. Opens like a door."

"Oh." Stevie stepped back and stared at the bookcase, and suddenly saw it as a door. Then everything became perfectly simple. He moved to its right edge, pushed firmly against the middle shelf, and let go. There was a muffled *click*, then, slowly and heavily, the bookcase swung outward into the room.

The next instant he was staggering backwards as Nels fell out of the opening, clutching at him as though he would never again let go. Together they went down, hard, gave simultaneous gasps and grunts, and began feebly and hysterically to giggle. Stevie was feeling so weak-kneed that he was glad to be on the floor instead of trying to stand up—and anyway, he was clinging to Nels as tightly as Nels was clinging to him. Nels was half-naked, and slippery with sweat, breathing in great panting gulps and sort of crying and shuddering, and half-laughing in little spurts.

"Gol," Stevie kept saying, in a strangled sort of voice because he couldn't seem to make his lungs work right. "Gol, Nels. I'm glad I came up here again. Gol, have you been in there all day?"

"All day," Nels whispered. "Tried to come back—keep promise."

"That's okay! I knew. I knew." Awkwardly, Stevie patted the slippery shoulder. "You sure are sweaty. How come you got in that closet?"

"Not a closet." Nels stirred, tried weakly to sit up free of Stevie—though he didn't loosen his clutch. "Yes—a closet. But more."

"More?" Stevie stared past Nels into the shadowed space visible beyond the half-opened bookcase.

"*Behind* closet," Nels said, in that hoarse, scratchy sort of whisper, and shivered. "Room."

"A *room*? Back there? What kind of room?"

"Don't know. Scary. Tower."

Stevie was beginning to wonder if Nels was okay. He talked so funny—and said such strange things. "What's the matter with your voice?" he asked uneasily as Nels gave a sort of choking cough.

"*Thirsty*."

"Oh! Well, *gol*, let me get you some water! I'll just run down to—"

"No! No." Nels clung to him fiercely. "Wait. Both go."

"But—okay, can you stand up, then?"

"Try."

Stevie's knees felt fairly normal now; he scrambled up, hampered by Nels's compulsive grip on him, and after some awkward stumbling, managed to get Nels up, too, and steady him while he got his balance.

"Still wobbly," Nels muttered apologetically, and shivered really hard. "Cold," he added.

"*Cold*? I think it's hot in here!" Stevie glanced back at the closet, suddenly realizing how hot it must have been in *there* all day. He caught a glimpse of something white behind the edge of the bookcase. "There's your shirt—want me to get it?"

"No! No, leave it. Get out of here now." Still clutching Stevie, Nels shrank away from the closet toward the door to the passage. He seemed unsteady but much stronger.

"What did you mean about a tower?" Stevie ventured.

"The secret. Tell you later—whole thing. Get a drink now."

"Oh, sure. Hey, there's a bathroom right here, across this little hall . . ." As he spoke, Stevie led the way across the passage and fumbled inside the door for a light switch. Somewhat to his surprise a dim light went on above the washbowl. "No drinking glass. But there's a cup! That'll do." He went on in, bringing Nels along because they were still tied together by Nels's grip on his sleeve, and reached for the cup to fill it at the faucet. Suddenly it was almost knocked from his hands by Nels's sharp recoil.

"No! Not that thing! How . . ."

"What's the matter?" Stevie exclaimed. Nels was staring at the cup as if it were a snake or something. Stevie stared at it himself, and it was just an ordinary teacup—a chipped, old one, with a pattern of roses.

"Let's go—go—other bathroom."

Nels was white as paper and tugging him to leave, so Stevie hastily set the cup down and came along. As they hurried out of the passage into the hall, he heard Aunt Ruth calling from the bottom of the back stairs.

"Stevie? Is that you up there, Stevie? Alice, what am I hearing? I thought—"

"It's me, Aunt Ruth!" Stevie yelled, and suddenly the queerness left and the ordinary world rushed back in, and it was today again—his awful birthday—and everybody was still down there searching for Nels. "I found him!" he sang out, and joy swept through him. "I found Nels! And he's okay, he's right here beside me!"

And then there were exclamations and hurried footsteps on the stairs, and everybody came running from everywhere.

There was no chance to be alone after that—not to talk—though Nels wouldn't let Stevie leave his side, not even for a second, not even when he took a bath. By the time they went down for the long-delayed birthday dinner he had quit clinging to Stevie's arm, but they sat with elbows touching as they ate, and stayed close beside each other the rest of the evening, and went up to bed right together.

Stevie could hardly remember back to the morning, getting out of this same bed with his mind full of ice cream bars. It seemed something from years ago—from a half-forgotten childhood. This was the longest day he had ever lived through —his very worst birthday. And his best.

NELS AWOKE in misery, having dreamed he was back in the closet. He sat up, tears starting to his eyes, then saw the flood of sunlight and the prosaic morning disorder of his and Stevie's room. Thankfully he sank back, feeling unreasonably as if he might cry anyway, and almost too weary to kick the covers off. It was going to be hot again—in fact it already was—but today there would be air. And water, and Cokes, and iced tea, and orange juice. *I'm all right*, he told himself. *I'm okay. It's over.*

"Nels?" came a tentative voice from the other bed. Stevie was propped up on one elbow, watching him carefully. "Hi," he added.

"Hi," said Nels, and smiled at him.

Stevie smiled back—broadly, gloriously; his whole face was suddenly alight. It occurred to Nels that it was the first time in weeks that he had seen Stevie *really* smile.

"I'm sure glad you're here. D'you feel okay?"

"Yeah, except I'm tired."

"Tired? When you just woke up?"

"Well, I mean sort of draggy. As if my arms and legs weighed a lot. I'll probably get over it pretty soon. Stevie?"

"Yeah?"

"Do you want to hear about—everything? I'll tell you now."

"Okay," Stevie breathed.

So Nels struggled up in bed, doubled his pillow with a vast effort, and sank back against it, letting his heavy arms lie bonelessly at either side. Then he began at the beginning.

It was harder than he'd expected. In the first place, he kept having to control his voice, which kept wanting to quaver or shake, or trail off because he suddenly felt he might cry, or go all breathy and gasping because there was all at once too much air in his lungs, or not enough, or something. And then it sounded so . . . silly, some of it, when he was trying to explain it out loud. Especially to Stevie, who kept asking wide-eyed, Stevie-like questions about the most ordinary details, things nobody else would pay attention to—such as how come Alan never wanted to play outside, or how come his mother never came in the store to buy groceries, or how come Nels never saw *any* other room but Alan's for maybe a week at first—didn't he ever have to go to the bathroom?

"Oh, don't be so *literal*!" Nels cried at last, feeling as though a terrier were at his heels.

"I'm sorry," Stevie said, looking stricken. "I only wondered."

"That's okay. I didn't mean to yell at you. It's only—well, it's hard to tell something when you keep asking questions." Especially when I can't answer them, Nels added to himself. That last question was making him very nervous. He kept remembering that rose-patterned cup Stevie had found in the east wing bathroom yesterday—and then shying away from the memory, as if . . . as if, far back in the shadowy corners of his mind, he knew things he didn't want to admit he knew.

"Nels?" Stevie ventured. "Go on. I won't ask anything else, I promise."

"No, don't promise that," Nels said abruptly. "Go ahead and ask whatever you want to. I think you'd better."

"I'd better? Why?"

"Because—oh, just because." Because you're my tether, Nels found himself thinking, without being quite sure what he meant. You keep pulling me back. To what's real.

But Alan was real too, wasn't he? Realer than those parents, who just disappeared—though never as real as Stevie, or Jenny, or Rory, or . . . Then were there degrees of being real? What do I mean by *real*? Nels asked himself in a kind of panic.

"Hey, Nels. Go on. Before everybody else wakes up and we have to go down to breakfast. Hey, did you ever ask Alan to come downstairs? Or in here or anything?"

"Oh, no." Nels paused to take a fresh breath and steady his

voice. "No, I don't think he could. I sort of had it figured out that he could go to the end of the east passage, but no farther."

"Only to there? What was keeping him from it?"

"I don't know. It was all sort of weird . . . I never did decide whether they were all ghosts, or leftover from some other time, or—"

"Gol! What d'you mean?"

Nels hesitated, then without much enthusiasm explained his pocket-of-time theory, which sounded singularly unconvincing to him now, while Stevie's eyes grew even ever rounder and more puzzled—and gradually, more uneasy. But he listened intently, interrupting only a few times, as Nels went on to describe the ciphers, and Alan's father's telescope, and the Spitfire and finally the spaceship.

"Wow, it must've been getting kind of crowded, wasn't it? In Alan's room?"

"Crowded?"

"Well, yeah, with all his regular furniture, and bed, and stuff, and then that Spitfire *and* a spaceship in the middle of the floor—"

"But the Spitfire wasn't there *then*."

"Oh. What happened to it?"

"Well, nothing. But it—" Nels hesitated. He seemed to be running out of breath again. "I suppose it was pulled up against the ceiling. I didn't notice." The fact was, he couldn't remember even missing it. It just suddenly—and conveniently—wasn't in the way. "I don't know," he muttered.

"But the spaceship's still there?" Stevie turned to stare at the east wall of there room as if he could see through it, through all the walls and rooms between. "It's there in Alan's room *right now*, waiting to be finished?"

"I don't *know*, you see. I suppose so. Unless it's gone. Maybe Alan's gone too. Maybe he's just disappeared. He might've,"

Nels insisted before Stevie could protest. "His father and mother both did."

"They *disappeared?*"

"Right before my eyes." It came out in a shuddery gasp, and he fell silent, turning cold with the memory of watching those smiling wax figures fade and vanish.

"Nels?" Stevie said after a minute in an odd, small voice. "Are you sure this—all *happened?* I mean, maybe you could've sort of dreamed it or something."

"Day after day? All day? When I wasn't even asleep?" Nels sat up and swung his legs over the edge of the bed, suddenly too restless to lie still any longer. "It must've happened—it must've. Only I don't know *how*. Let's get up or something."

"Okay." Stevie was out of bed at once, reaching for his T-shirt. "Are your legs and arms still heavy?"

"No, they're okay. Listen, I'll *prove* it happened. I'll show you the door to that—that room with the stairway. Then you'll know I didn't make it up."

Stevie looked at him quickly. "I never said you made it up."

"Well, whatever you said. Come on, get your clothes on." Nels began to dress hastily.

"You mean we'll go right now?" Stevie snatched up his jeans eagerly, and flapped them right side out.

"It's our only chance, isn't it? Aunt Ruth said she was going to nail that bookcase shut first thing after breakfast."

Stevie halted, one leg in his jeans. "Hey, she did. Hey, Nels—we have to stop her, don't we? She'll nail Alan up inside!"

Nels met his uneasy, puzzled look with one of his own, then turned away without speaking. The only answer in his mind was *That suits me, let her!* But he didn't say it. Instead he opened the bedroom door, listened a moment to the early morning silence of the house, then waited till Stevie was close beside him. They walked barefoot down the stealthily creaking hall to the carved screen, keeping their elbows touching.

In the passage Nels stopped, suddenly so sure he would see Alan in the mirror on the General's door that he was unable to move, almost unable to breathe for a moment. But something stronger than his dread was forcing him on.

And after all there was nobody in the mirror, or in the General's room. The bookcase was closed, exactly as he had first seen it all those weeks ago. Exactly as if it wouldn't really open at all. But it would. Oh, it opened! He hadn't dreamed yesterday.

Without giving himself a chance to think about it, Nels stepped up to the shelves, pressed, then shrank back to Stevie's side as the bookcase swung ponderously ajar. After a moment he said in an almost-steady voice, "You know, I was thinking we left it open last night."

"Aunt Ruth came in here and closed it. When you were having your bath." Stevie craned his neck to peer inside. "I guess she picked up your shirt, too. There's only some paper and junk. Nels, where's the other door? To the weird room?"

"In the back wall. You can only see a crack, sort of outlining it."

Cautiously, Stevie moved forward, poked his head into the opening for a long moment, then withdrew it and looked at Nels. "I don't—see it. Any crack, or anything."

"Right directly in front of you! Here, I'll—" Nels stepped close enough to swing the bookcase a little wider, so that the early morning sunlight shone full inside.

And there wasn't any crack in the back wall. It was a solid sheet of plywood, old, discolored along one side, but whole and uncut. Nels stared frantically, until his eyes felt wide and strained—he even put one foot inside the closet, clinging fast to Stevie with the other hand, so that he could run exploratory fingers all across the blank space where the door should be. The yardstick still leaned against a corner. Near it—and Nels was suddenly staring there instead—was a little clutter of paper, the yellow kind like the pad on the General's desk, and a plastic cleaner's bag, and a scrap of red cellophane, and two books. One was the General's cipher book; the other, with a pebbly dark green cover, was the astronomy book he thought of as Alan's father's. It had a paper sticking out of it on which he could clearly see the fanblades of his spaceship sketch.

Slowly Nels backed out of the closet, his mind in a turmoil except for one dawning, unthinkable question: *Did* I make it up, then? Just sit there day after day and invent the whole thing, like some horrible game?

"Nels?" said Stevie uneasily.

Nels seized the edge of the bookcase and swung it shut, pushed hard until he heard the *click*. "I can't see it either," he said as steadily as he could, though his voice wanted to veer wildly in all directions. "It just isn't there now. The door must've . . . sealed itself up. Yes, that's it. It disappeared, like Alan's parents. Now there isn't any way at all to get into the tower."

"I've never even noticed that tower from outside," Stevie confessed. "I mean, I must've seen it. But I just never noticed it."

"Well, *it's* still there, it's got to be. It's part of the building. Come on, I'll show you. I want to get out of here anyhow—and never come back."

He led the way quickly out of the General's room and the east wing, and across the hall to the back stairs. Alice had arrived by now, to start breakfast; they managed to slip out the squeaky back door while she was rattling dishes in the pantry, ran across the service yard and started down the driveway, peering up.

"Kitchen roof's in the way," Nels said. "We'll have to get

around to the front, and back off almost to the road—that's where I saw it first."

But he couldn't find the right spot. Something was always in the way—the dining room roof overhang, the big fir tree. They ended by crossing the road, picking their barefoot way gingerly over the gravel, and scrambling up the little embankment. And there Nels had to face it, because he could see the whole roofline plainly.

There was no tower on the Inn.

For a long time he stood silent, his gaze first raking back and forth along the roof ridge, then settling reluctantly on the little ornamental turret which thrust up above the dining room. It was no bigger than a chimney. Yet his memory showed him the tower rising there solid and real, with that same witch's-hat roof and fancy shingling and new-moon weathervane, but *big*, like the tower in Alan's puzzle—big enough for rooms, and half a dozen windows—one of them the window from which he had so often watched Stevie pedaling along the road. *What if he should look up here some time?* he had asked once, and Alan had said, *He wouldn't see a thing.* Now I don't see a thing, Nels thought. But *surely* I did then? It was real!—only what do I mean by "real"?

For an instant, he felt deprived, forlorn—as if his life were suddenly as empty as those vanished rooms. Then he was remembering the cinnamon toast breakfast that pearly morning in the blue and white kitchen, and Alan begging him to stay. Stay! Stay shut up in a suffocating closet, forever? The danger had turned out to be real enough.

With a long, convulsive shudder, Nels looked away from the Inn, from the tower in his memory, and met Stevie's anxious eyes. Then he stared down at his bare feet, close beside Stevie's smaller ones in the coarse late summer grass. "Listen," he said. "Don't tell anybody any of this. Just don't ever say anything about it. Okay?"

"Okay," Stevie muttered softly.

"They'd think I was crazy."

There was a long silence, during which a grasshopper suddenly spurted out of a weed clump and sailed away on stiff thin wings.

"Nels?" said Stevie. "D'you think you were, sort of? For a while? I mean, you acted awful funny."

"I don't know," Nels repeated for what seemed the hundredth time that morning, and had to stop once more to get his lungs working and his voice back under control. "What's more, I don't want to know," he added. "I just don't want to think about it, ever again."

"Okay," Stevie agreed quickly, in a relieved tone. "I don't either. Just so it's over."

"Well, it's over. Yesterday ended it."

"Then let's go eat breakfast and start on something better."

Nels couldn't help a rather choked laugh—it sounded so exactly like Stevie—and right away the world began to seem more normal. *He* always knows what's real, he reflected as they started limping and hopping back across the road. If I just hang onto Stevie I'll be all right.

His hand reached out of itself and touched Stevie's shirt, grasped a fold of it just lightly, so Stevie wouldn't feel that something was dragging at him—though he had not complained about all this clinging, but simply accepted Nels's need. I'll get over it pretty soon, Nels told himself, a little ashamed. But he didn't dare lose contact with Stevie, even physically—not yet—and he knew he'd never again allow them to be separated for long. Stevie was never mixed-up about what was real—and he never thought he could get out of facing up to it somehow. He just stood and let it hit him, and let it hurt. And that was better than hiding, Nels thought fervently. It was painful but it was better than ending up a prisoner for good.

After breakfast, when he and Stevie were heading toward Parker's meadow with the new insect net and a jar with air holes punched in the lid, he blurted, "I wish summer was over. I wish it was time to leave Reeves Ferry tomorrow."

"Oh, well," Stevie said. "It isn't bad here. *Now,*" he added. "Besides, when we go home . . . Oh, never mind. Skip it."

"No. I want to talk about it."

Stevie glanced at him. "You never did before."

"I do now," Nels said doggedly.

"Well—I just meant—when we go home we don't know where we'll *be* or anything. Or who with. I mean, it'll be okay I guess. Other kids' parents get divorced and they get used to it. But I just—I keep worrying about it. I can't quit."

"Me neither," Nels admitted. And I'm not going to try, he thought, almost with relief. Worrying about the divorce was better than refusing to think of it. Even deciding which parent to live with was better. Anything real was better. And anyhow . . . in the space of two swishing steps through the tall, coarse grass, he realized his decision was behind him. His mind was already made up and it would stay made up, no matter what happened, or what anybody said. "I know one thing," he told Stevie firmly. "We'll be together—us kids. I'll never leave you and Rory and Jenny—not till we're all grown-up."

"Leave us?" Stevie stopped short and stared at him.

"Dad wanted me to come to Alaska with him. But I'm not going."

"*Alaska?*" Stevie whispered. "Gol, is Dad going to Alaska? What's he going to—"

"I guess he's going to try being a bush pilot. See if it works out."

"Then won't he ever be coming back here? To live?—And he was going to take *you?*" Stevie fell silent, gazing at Nels, with the dawn of comprehension in his face rapidly spreading to full daylight. "I guess you wanted to go," he said huskily after a minute. "I wouldn't blame you. I mean—you'll miss him worst."

"Never mind." So I'll miss him, Nels thought, making himself stare straight at it. So it'll hurt. So okay, it'll just have to *hurt*, till I get over it. And I'll get over it because people *do* . . . Somewhere inside of him, he could feel the words taking hold, forming a thin protective sheath, like a muscle he didn't know he had. "Never mind. That's not important." Nels waved it away, suddenly sure what was important, and full of a need to make Stevie see it too. "All us kids have got to *stay together*, that's the big thing. We've got to *promise* each other. If we stick together, then whatever happens outside—whatever the grown-ups do—it won't matter so much. D'you see? We'll still be *us*."

After a moment, Stevie nodded slowly, and his face lost its troubled look. "Well, gol, *I'll* promise. It suits me fine."

"It suits me fine too," Nels said, and for the first time all summer felt himself begin to settle down, inside, and smooth out a little. They walked on, shirt sleeves just touching, toward the outcrop of rocks Stevie was so set on. The meadow was alive with grasshoppers, buzzing and whirring with their song. And Nels suddenly felt it the best thing in the world to be doing, and the most solidly important—just to be collecting insects for Stevie's zoo.

Eloise McGraw